LOVING HARPER

SEAL Brotherhood: Silver Team

Book 2

SHARON HAMILTON

SHARON HAMILTON'S BOOK LIST

SEAL BROTHERHOOD BOOKS

SEAL BROTHERHOOD SERIES

Accidental SEAL Book 1

Fallen SEAL Legacy Book 2

SEAL Under Covers Book 3

SEAL The Deal Book 4

Cruisin' For A SEAL Book 5

SEAL My Destiny Book 6

SEAL of My Heart Book 7

Fredo's Dream Book 8

SEAL My Love Book 9

SEAL Encounter Prequel to Book 1

SEAL Endeavor Prequel to Book 2

Ultimate SEAL Collection Vol. 1 Books 1-4 / 2 Prequels

Ultimate SEAL Collection Vol. 2 Books 5-9

SEAL BROTHERHOOD LEGACY SERIES

Watery Grave Book 1

Honor The Fallen Book 2

Grave Injustice Book 3

Deal With The Devil Book 4

Cruisin' For Love Book 5

Destiny of Love Book 6

Heart of Gold Book 7

Father's Dream Book 8

Second Time Love Book 9

Little Miracles Novella

SEAL BROTHERHOOD SILVER TEAM SERIES

Something About Silver Book 1

Loving Harper Book 2

BAD BOYS OF SEAL TEAM 3 SERIES

SEAL's Promise Book 1

SEAL My Home Book 2

SEAL's Code Book 3

Big Bad Boys Bundle Books 1-3

BAND OF BACHELORS SERIES

Lucas Book 1

Alex Book 2

Jake Book 3

Jake 2 Book 4

Big Band of Bachelors Bundle

BONE FROG BROTHERHOOD SERIES

New Year's SEAL Dream Book 1

SEALed At The Altar Book 2

SEALed Forever Book 3

SEAL's Rescue Book 4

SEALed Protection Book 5

Bone Frog Brotherhood Superbundle

BONE FROG BACHELOR SERIES

Bone Frog Bachelor Book 0.5

Unleashed Book 1

Restored Book 2

Revenge Book 3

Legacy Book 4

SUNSET SEALS SERIES

SEALed at Sunset Book 1

Second Chance SEAL Book 2

Treasure Island SEAL Book 3

Escape to Sunset Book 4

The House at Sunset Beach Book 5

Second Chance Reunion Book 6

Love's Treasure Book 7

Finding Home Book 8

Sunset SEALs Duet #1

Sunset SEALs Duet #2

LOVE VIXEN

Bone Frog Love

SHADOW SEALS

Shadow of the Heart

Shadow Warrior

Midnight Bite Book 4

THE GUARDIANS
Heavenly Lover Book 1
Underworld Lover Book 2
Underworld Queen Book 3
Redemption Book 4

FALL FROM GRACE SERIES
Gideon: Heavenly Fall

SUNSET BEACH SERIES
I'll Always Love You
Back To You

NOVELLAS
SEAL Of Time: Trident Legacy

All of Sharon's books are available on Audible,
narrated by the talented J.D. Hart.

ABOUT THE BOOK

Shattered Dreams Become Second-Chance Real Love...

After surviving a sniper's bullet in North Africa, Lydia Cunningham is back in Sonoma County, piecing together her life with Harper, the man she once loved deeply. The challenge? Her memories of their past are lost and fragmented, yet her feelings for Harper are sprinting ahead of her slow-returning recall. It's a race between her heart and her memory, and she's not sure which will cross the finish line first.

Harper, now leading the elite Silver Team, is caught up in a whirlwind of dangerous missions, making it tough to be the partner Lydia needs. Meanwhile, the emergence of a newly-formed terrorist cell uncovered nearby, now targeting Lydia, adds danger to their lives.

As they navigate the treacherous waters of reconciliation and rediscovery, Lydia and Harper confront the true meaning of love and sacrifice. In this gripping second book in the SEAL Brotherhood: Silver Team series, their love will be tested to the breaking point. Is the journey towards healing a cost too dear to pay if it demands the ultimate sacrifice?

AUTHOR'S NOTE

I always dedicate my SEAL Brotherhood books to the brave men and women who defend our shores and keep us safe. Without their sacrifice and that of their families—because a warrior's fight always includes his or her family—I wouldn't have the freedom and opportunity to make a living writing these stories. They sometimes pay the ultimate price so we can debate, argue, go have coffee with friends, raise our children, and see them have children of their own.

One of my favorite tributes to warriors resides on many memorials, including one I saw honoring the fallen of WWII on an island in the Pacific:

> "When you go home
> Tell them of us, and say,
> For your tomorrow,
> We gave our today."

These are my stories created out of my own imagination. Anything that is inaccurately portrayed is either my mistake or done intentionally to disguise something I might have overheard over a beer or in the corner of one of the hangouts along the Coronado Strand.

I support two main charities. Navy SEAL/UDT Museum operates in Ft. Pierce, Florida. Please learn about this wonderful museum, all run by active and former SEALs and their friends and families, and who rely on public support, not that of the United States Government.

www.navysealmuseum.org

IF YOU GOT ANY CLOSER, YOU WOULD HAVE TO ENLIST

I also support Wounded Warriors, who tirelessly bring together the warrior as well as the family members who are just learning to deal with their soldier's condition and have nowhere to turn. It is a long path to becoming well, but I've seen first-hand what this organization does for its warriors and the families who love them. Please give what your heart tells you is right. If you cannot give, volunteer at one of the many service centers all over the United States. Get involved. Do something meaningful for someone who gave so much of themselves, to families who have paid the price for your freedom. You'll find a family there unlike any other on the planet.

www.woundedwarriorproject.org

CHAPTER 1

H ARPER WAS COMING home today after a month-long deployment. Butterflies filled Lydia's stomach, and her nerves were on edge. She didn't know whether to be elated or concerned. She wondered how her reaction would stand up to the Lydia he used to know when he came home from overseas as part of SEAL Team 3. Her memory of their relationship was still mired in distant fog. The picture wasn't getting any clearer, either.

Lydia had worked with Harper for several weeks after her original return to the house where they'd lived in Santa Rosa, Sonoma County, California. This was all designed to prepare her for his next deployment. She needed to be fully self-sufficient while he was away. For the first time, he had taken on a mission and left her in charge, alone, other than the short trips to Washington, D.C. This one would be longer and could take him out of the country.

Other times, if he had to stay in D.C. for more than an overnight, he had a member of his team stay back with her. Sally, their neighbor down the driveway, had also become a "new to Lydia" trusted friend. Harper told her stories about how she and Sally were close before her unfortunate attempted murder.

Armed with Harper's patient guidance and training, Lydia now felt comfortable being out in public and driving herself back-and-forth to the store, most of the time with Venom in tow. She relied on the handsome Doberman, who seemed to up his level of concern whenever the two of them were alone, as if he knew the circumstances of her past. She did remember more about him than she did Harper, which had been a sore subject with Harper, although he tried not to show it. It had, unfortunately, been their last conversation before he flew down to Coronado to leave with the rest of his team.

"Venom, you stay here and watch the car for Mama, okay?" She rolled down the windows and calculated she wouldn't have to leave the car AC running. There was enough room for him to jump out, if he needed to. It would be their mistake if anyone tried to put their arm inside the car to try to steal it. She could feel the dog's eyes on her back. It was reassuring.

She brought Venom with her on her shopping

sprees, mostly because Harper insisted the dog would be alert to things Lydia was not yet aware of.

Lydia liked to shop in a high-end grocery store that carried organic foods and meats, but Harper complained bitterly about the prices. Still, figuring it was part of her healing process, she took to getting healthy, clean food items and considered it an investment in their future.

She'd tried, but even the organic foods and clean living didn't do anything to bring back those lost memories. There were little glimpses of it here and there, flashes of memories, mostly surrounding Venom or their flower garden. But the full weight and depth of their relationship was still lost to her.

Today, Harper was returning, and it was her custom to make him a fresh pie and get him one of his favorite cuts of meat, a two-inch thick ribeye steak. She didn't try to compete with him on the barbecue, that was all Harper territory, but she could find the nicest, most marbled and well-aged piece of meat they had. The butcher knew exactly what she wanted and frequently held things aside for her when he expected her. After picking up the meat, she glanced at the dairy section and then down into the condiments, picking up green olives that she just could not get enough off, imported from Spain. Harper had said she hadn't appeared to like them before. Now, she had to have a handful just about every day.

She grabbed some half-and-half for their coffee and some fresh pomegranate seeds, tangelos, and bananas. Harper was threatening to plant bananas in their backyard, but it wasn't quite warm enough. Over the summer, they planned to try growing them anyway.

Since he loved her brand of cornbread, something she learned in Italy where she added creamed corn, pimento, and hot peppers to the batter, she picked up four boxes of inexpensive pre-prepared mix. It was their favorite form of dessert.

Each time she went out, especially when she had Venom, she learned more and more about the community, the people she used to know and hang with, even getting reacquainted with Sally. The older and very fit woman had been a great help at first in coaching her to understand all the stages of grief Harper had gone through when he'd been told she had been killed. Sally had been there right at his side, his quirky grandmotherly-like neighbor who wouldn't give him quarter, arguing with him any chance she could. It was her form of tough love, never bestowed on Lydia, but thrown at Harper all the time.

While she wandered down the fruit section, choosing the greenest bananas she could find, she noticed a couple pushing a cart with a child seat strapped to the top where a toddler would sit. But upon careful study, as they were facing the opposite direction, she didn't think the swaddling appeared like a real child was inside. The size and shape looked all wrong, for some reason.

She even considered perhaps they had a small puppy in the padded seat.

It continued to bother her. She observed them at a distance while shopping, hoping to string out her spree long enough so she could follow them in the checkout line or perhaps find them leaving the store to be able to take a picture of their car license plate. Harper was big on getting license plates so that he could run them by his buddies in D.C.

The clerk at the bakery department offered her a fresh piece of rye bread with sesame seeds and onion chips all over the crust. It was Harper's favorite, although Lydia wasn't very fond of onions or garlic. She took a bite and wrinkled her nose but nodded.

"I'll take two. I think he'll love that."

"You better get some more butter. He's gonna want to have a gob of butter on every slice. He tells me he spreads it like peanut butter," the baker said.

"Yes, I know, but he's changing some of his diet. He won't always be a man of action, and those years are bound to catch up to him eventually. I don't want my guy to look pregnant."

He laughed. "Not Harper. Never Harper. Maybe

you, my dear—I mean getting pregnant—but Harper will be working out into his eighties, I'm sure. It's a religion with him. His body's a temple and all that. Besides, he has to work out to burn all the calories he eats."

"I think he's got a little tad bit of a belly on him. He tries to hide it." She laughed. "You know that in five years he'll be fifty." She was only repeating what she'd been told. She honestly didn't remember how old he was. It dampened her mood a bit.

To cheer her up, the baker added, "Well, guys don't count after forty. They can't wait to be old enough to drink, take a girl out, go to bars, and drive a racy car. Then after they get old enough, they can't wait to go back to being a kid again. I think the older these guys come home, the more likely they are to just revert back to their high school or college days. My brother was a SEAL, graduated in the class five years after Harper. He was a big help too."

"Really? I didn't know that."

"Yup."

"Does he live here in Sonoma County?" she asked him.

"Ma'am, he didn't make it home. Afghanistan. No place to die."

Lydia was glad Harper wasn't doing the Middle East tours any longer, not that what he did wasn't dangerous. "I'm so sorry." She began to tear up.

"He loved every minute of it. Harder on us than it was on him. He didn't suffer. But I remember when he came back after his first deployment. They get serious while they first start out on the teams, but by the time they're done and they've put in their ten or twenty years, they're downright high school football players. All of Derrick's buddies have stayed close with the family. We're grateful we have them."

The baker had spoken to her earlier about how long Harper had shopped with him, when he used to head the bakery department at a big box store. She was so sorry she didn't remember him at all from before.

He threw in some chocolate-glazed donuts Harper liked for free and waved her off to help the next customer.

Lydia checked out, and as she did so, she scanned the aisles back-and-forth, and then she studied the parking lot, looking for some evidence that the couple in the store had followed her out. But she didn't see anybody of interest, made it to her car, opened the rear hatch with her lower leg, and set her groceries inside. She already had vanilla ice cream for the pie she was going to make for Harper at home. It was a warm late spring day, so she was glad she didn't have to worry about it melting. She was going to stop by and take a look at one of her favorite nurseries on the way home.

She headed down Matanzas Creek Road to a boutique nursery that had been burned out in the fires several years ago but had rebuilt. They first began in the garage and driveway of the owner's house, but eventually, they were able to convert the house to a full-on nursery with ample parking. They carried gorgeous varieties of seasonal flowers and shrubs, some vegetables to add to their population at home, and bulbs of all sizes and varieties when in season.

Lydia took Venom on his leash, and together, they walked through the row of fruit trees that had just began bearing tiny fruits, a couple of the pear and apple trees had blossoms barely brown enough to fall to the ground, fully fertilized and ready for the fruiting phase. She scanned the berry bushes and wondered if Harper would like her to get more blackberries but held off.

Over her shoulder, she noticed a car drive into the parking lot, and to her dismay, the male of the couple in the store got out of the driver's side and started walking through the office, heading out toward the nursery beyond. He was coming toward Lydia. She bent over, giving Venom a heads-up. He alerted right away, ever attuned to that command.

"Ready, Venom?" she whispered as the dog looked up at her adoringly. "Watch. Guard Mama, okay?"

Venom looked deep into her eyes, then searched

around him, and, within seconds, locked on the gentleman approaching them. He wore leather sandals. His feet crunched the crushed granite as he made it down the pathway toward them.

Lydia didn't have to say anything to the dog. He had been given the alert, and as the gentleman got within twenty feet of them, Venom started to growl, and then he barked.

The man, just a little older than a boy, really, had dark hair long enough to wear in a ponytail. She noted a sleeve of tats on his arms and some large swaths of islander tats on his calves.

"Whoa, whoa! You got yourself a vicious dog there," he said, appearing almost too casual. Lydia could tell he was legitimately scared, and for good reason.

"Oh, don't mind him. He's just hungry." She grinned and saw her comment had the desired effect.

The man stepped back suddenly. "Hungry? So he wants to take a bite out of me, is that what you're saying?"

"I guess he figures you smell good. Do you smell good?" she asked him. "You know Dobermans never forget a scent. Never."

The stranger was going to say something, but Venom lunged in his direction, which was not what he was supposed to do. It took all the strength Lydia had to hold the dog back. If it wasn't for the fact that he had a choker collar on, she would not have been able to.

"Venom. Venom, stop." She avoided saying the part about that it was okay or that he's a friend. She just told him to stop. So Venom did just that. He sat immediately and never took his eyes off the gentleman. Every time the fellow looked back at Venom, the dog showed his teeth and whispered a growl.

Lydia decided to wander a little more since Venom had already tracked the gentleman, and if she really needed his help, she would let him go and pin the guy somewhere. He was trained not to hurt, unless he was struck. At least until it was time for somebody else to restrain him. She wasn't going to do that, of course.

They wandered back and forth through the fruit trees and bushy shrubs, but Venom looked around every tree and every bush they walked past, making sure he kept track of wherever the gentleman walked. Finally, after about fifteen minutes, he walked back through the office and out into the parking lot where she saw him get in his SUV, say something to his female passenger she recognized from the store, and take off.

She considered what Harper would do, had started to think like him. What had she learned? First, the couple probably had her license plate, so it would be easy for them to find where she lived if they had any kind of contacts in law enforcement or security. They knew two places she shopped, so perhaps she'd have to alter that routine. And she knew Venom had already recognized him as a possible threat and would do so again, because the dog never forgot a scent, and if he was instructed, he would do his ultimate to protect her. That wasn't really her biggest concern.

Her biggest concern was what would happen if Harper and Venom were gone and she was left alone.

CHAPTER 2

H ARPER'S HULKING FRAME filled the doorway as he swung it open, catching her midway between the kitchen and the living room area. She hadn't heard him drive up. Venom was by her side and then dashed into Harper's arms.

He dropped his duty bag with a loud metallic thud then let loose another backpack just inside the doorway just as Venom lunged up at him. He quickly knelt to receive the hundred-plus pound Doberman. Looking tired and dusty from a long trip, he gave her a wink, while he occupied the large pup and tried not to sprawl all over the floor at her feet.

"Venom, that was one of the best loves I've ever gotten. You're such a sweetheart. Ever faithful, aren't you?" he said as he hugged the dog around the neck and let him lick his face and neck and hands, Venom jumping and barking as he turned circles in front of and all around Harper, showing how excited he was for the return.

Remaining on his knees, Harper continued but spoke to Lydia, "You know dogs are the only animal around that the later you are the more excited they are for you to be home, right?"

"Oh, I think he's excited about everything. He just likes having us around. But especially you, Harper, of course.

Harper stood and adjusted his back with a loud crack, left the bags, managed two long strides to cross the rest of the distance, and took her in his arms.

"How's my girl? You miss me?"

She peeled herself from his frontside. "What the hell do you think?"

"Oh, so now she's swearing. That's my old Lydia."

She laughed. "I've been spending time with Sally."

"And she got it from me," he answered.

"Hardly. I think she was well on her way to swearing like a sailor before you even met her. But I'm not wanting to argue, Sweetheart. Welcome home." She kissed him again.

The thought of missing Harper and the long nights without his huge muscled body next to hers, making her feel small and insignificant and fully protected by his hulking frame, it made her weak at the knees.

"That's what every warrior wants to hear. The best two words in the English language."

"I could hardly stand it. It was a long month, Harper. Will they always be this long?"

"Enough of the questions. How's my girl?" he asked again and then gave her another kiss.

Her hands traveled up his shoulders to his thick neck and into his hair as she squeezed him. She pressed and melted into him—every hard and muscled ripple of his flesh. She smelled his musky man scent, the most delicious aroma in the world.

"Nervous." She surprised herself with the comment.

His eyes got wide. "Nervous? You? You're fearless."

"You know. It's all still so new to me, Harper. I feel like we just met. You have all those memories of how we were together, and…"

His low growl did affect the moisture in her panties.

"I have lots of memories of that, Sweetheart," he whispered. "You just need to relax and let me do all the lovin', babe. You don't have to do a thing but enjoy. I'll show you. I'll show you everything. We'll take it slow," and then he lowered his voice even more, "and intense, 'til you don't know if you can handle it. I'd love to blow your mind and take you to new places or places you've been before but don't remember." He kissed the side of her face, her ear, then tilted her chin and kissed her fully on the lips.

She surrendered to him. Let his callused hands roam over her body, claiming it, owning her, holding her by a small tether as he flew them both across the sky, until her knees wobbled and her sex bulged and began to pulse. He whispered, "Love you, Lydia. Tell me to stop if you have to, but, Baby, I've been dreaming about this for a whole month. I started dreaming about it on the flight down to Coronado."

She was tingling, and then her body began to shake. Her breath was ragged. She squealed when his fingers found their way inside her panties. She started to stop him, and then he placed his forehead next to hers and watched her eyes as he inserted those persistent fingers slowly inside her, daring her to make him stop.

The center of her universe begged for him to go deep. He commanded her lips as his fingers coaxed her opening to prepare her for the next chapter. He had never been so arduous, so tender and demanding, insisting she ratchet up her free spirit and let go, let him help her soar.

Then she remembered dinner.

"I have steaks. I have—"

"I want to fuck you, Lydia. Maybe we'll have it for breakfast. What do you say?"

"Was it always like this, when—"

He placed his hand over her mouth. "Yessss. It was always hot, like this. You liked it hot. So hot I couldn't stand it. Did you know that?"

She sighed, wrapped in his arm while his other hand did his bidding, claiming her riches and preparing her so that there wouldn't be a chance in the world she'd tell him to stop. "Just let go, Lydia. Be mine. Be completely mine."

"Am I as hot—"

He covered her mouth again then kissed her. "Better. You're hotter. You're like a virgin. You're more innocent. I love it. Give me more. Practice anything you want on me, Sweetheart."

"I get embarrassed."

"You like this? Do you like how this feels?" he asked as he inserted deeply. "Tell me. Say the words."

"I love you, Harper."

"No, not those words."

She was losing it. Nearly delirious and full of honey-sweet heat. She did not have the memory of how they used to be together, but the Lydia today wanted him more than she'd ever wanted anything before in her life. She wanted to be consumed by him, wanted him to play her body like an instrument, make her his servant as he served her back.

"Say the words, Sweetheart," he said as he dipped his head and nuzzled inside her shirt. "I need to hear it."

She thought longer, and then the clarity came to

her. She wanted to match his intensity, let him command her. She knew what she had to say next. After that, there would never be any turning back.

"Fuck me."

CHAPTER 3

T HE NIGHT WAS rough between them. They were urgent for each other. The bedsheets and blankets were twisted and strewn all over the sides. Sometimes they'd dive under and explore in the dark. He lapped at her sex and made her come so many times she began to lose count, which was the point.

Her nipples ached to the rhythm of the steady pulse deep inside her demanding release. Her swollen lips hurt as he sucked and kissed them, his fingers pinching her nub and making her jump. He played with her for precious, painful minutes each time she demanded he enter her, trying to draw him up on top of her by his hips.

He laughed as she moaned and showed her need. He leaned over her, kissing a ring from ear to ear, under her chin, as his fingers pressed his member back and forth, teasing her with his hardness, her juices covering him.

He placed her knees over his shoulders, raising her pelvis up with his powerful hands, pressing her nub with both thumbs, then inserting them one by one, in and out, until her legs began to shake. He tucked his knees under her buttocks, her sex spread wide for him as he took her in his mouth, driving her insane with desire.

One hand guided him to her opening, and then he stopped.

"The words. I must hear the words, my love."

She arched up, using her legs on his shoulders as a lever as she raised her lower torso up higher. "Fuck me, Harper. Please. Fuck me!"

He was inside her in a flash, deep and rooting deeper. His guttural groveling turning her bones to rubber. His in and out motions came in waves. Her crescendo grew again, this time not a mini climax, but one big, long rolling one.

But he stopped suddenly. He pulled one of her legs over his head, turning her on her tummy, angling to fuck her sideways. He grabbed a pillow and placed it under her belly. One hand reached around her waist to capture her bud again, relentlessly squeezing and pressing it until she felt the crescendo grow again. Her ears buzzed. She felt the streams of sweat roll down her back as she drove her head into the pillow below and raised her butt up on the air as he plunged deeper still, picking up the pace.

He was splitting her in two, and she didn't want him to stop. He held her hips up, making himself a solid platform of her ass as he worked her insides with fierce abandon. She could hardly breathe.

And then she began to explode, grabbing the pillow and screaming into it. Somewhere in the distance, she heard him saying, "Yes, Baby. Let yourself go. Yes. Yes. Just let it fall, Sweetheart."

He bent down and kissed her right ear, "Here we go, Baby. You and me, Baby. Together."

He lurched forward but then pressed into her quivering sex as she held him tight with her internal muscles, milking every last drop. He was so deep; the dull ache of his member against her womb was the pleasure-pain she'd sought. His fingers sifted through her hair, waiting for her climax to slowly melt, waiting for their frantic breaths to steady. He blew cool air at the nape of her neck, and the entire length of her spine tingled with desire again.

And then all she wanted to do was kiss him. Do it all over again. She held his hands as they squeezed her breasts. She was limp like a rag doll, all his.

And he definitely belonged to her. Fully.

THEY TOOK A catnap, and then Harper scampered downstairs to feed Venom. He brought up some grapes and tangelos they had in the kitchen, along with an ice-cold bottle of water.

Propped up against the damp pillows, they ate in silence, sharing the water and feeding each other grapes one by one. He broke apart the tangelo and threw the peels over the edge of the bed, the light citrus fragrance refreshing, even stimulating.

He fed her the remaining four grapes in her palm, ate the tangelo slices she was going to eat, then lay his head down against her chest, and listened to her heart.

Everything felt so natural between them. But it was also exciting. For her, she was exploring this man, his prowess (and she had no doubts about that even before their first night together), the way he rocked her world and then even demanded more. It only made her want to give in to him over and over again.

Their lovemaking continued in the shower as he took her from behind, pressing her breasts and face against the cool tile surface, bending his knees and having her ride his cock as the warm water sprayed and then turned cold.

"I'm going to have to get a bigger water heater, I guess," he whispered to the side of her face as they finished. She washed him in the cold water, using his overspray to clean herself.

In large fluffy towels, they dried off, just in time for round four.

AROUND MIDNIGHT, VENOM stirred on the bed and sat erect with his ears extended, listening. Then he barked.

She thought about the strange couple she'd seen at the store today and was going to say something when Harper leapt out of bed and put on his boxers. Grabbing his SIG Sauer from the nightstand, he took off downstairs, following Venom.

Lydia wrapped the fluffy towel she was lying on around her and slipped downstairs to watch. She saw the flashlight washing back and forth on the rear deck, then down the stairs and into the garden. She checked the front door, noting it was indeed locked, and pressed her face against the glass of the side window. There was no moon tonight, so with little light, she couldn't make out anything, except for Harper's massive pickup and her SUV. She thought she saw a shadow cross the porch, but then it disappeared. A broken branch lay on the brick walkway. The wind was blowing a gloomy howl.

She walked back toward the kitchen and heard Venom barking furiously. Harper was trying to keep up as the dog ran up the back steps and skirted the edge of the house, headed to the front, as fast as his legs could carry him. He was chasing something.

When she peered outside the window again, she saw the Doberman pacing back and forth, telling off the stars and scolding the moon for not being there. He snarled, twirled in fury, signaling he was on high alert and waiting for instructions. Harper joined him, and she could hear him asking questions of the dog.

He was given the command to fetch. Venom took off down the driveway all the way to the security gate that was closing in front of him.

She realized someone had just passed through their gate. That meant they also got past the gate down by the road. The intruders had a passcode to use.

Her heart sank.

She listened in the quiet as Venom galloped back toward Harper and the front porch. He was examining tire marks in the crushed granite, searching for anything that might have been left as far as a clue.

Finally, looking completely ridiculous in his red, white, and blue boxers and blue flip-flops, he brought Venom to the front door and knocked for her to let them inside. He slipped off his flip-flops before entering.

"Did you see anything?" she asked.

"I just missed him, I guess. Venom acted like he recognized the scent. How odd."

"They made it out the gate. I saw it closing behind."

"Them? You saw two people?"

"No, but I have something to tell you. At the store today, I spotted a couple who looked odd." She told him about her incident and about Venom scaring the man at the nursery later. "I'm sorry I didn't tell you."

"We got a little carried away," he said with a sly smile, starting to unpeel the towel from her body. "Just what are you hiding in there?" he said curiously.

"So they have the combination, then."

"Easy to fix. Unless I have a mole on my team, impossible to guess at. I'll have to change the codes tomorrow." He stared back at her in the nightness. He was breathing hard, and so was she. Her heart fluttered, partly from the excitement, partly because he was rubbing her rear end through the towel.

"Do you think it's safe?" she asked.

"I think so, for now. Venom has made his announcement. Someone would be foolish not to have taken note."

"What about Sally? Should we call her?" Lydia asked.

"Good idea." He grabbed his cell, left charging in the bathroom, and dialed her number. Lydia heard the angry squawk on the other end. Of course, they'd awakened her.

"This better be good," Sally said.

"Are you secure? We just had an intruder, got through the gates. Venom picked him up."

"Up at your place?"

"Yup. Are you all locked up?"

"I am. How the hell did he get inside?"

"We'll have to change the gate codes."

"Hell yeah. I think I'm going to go down to the Humane Society and get me a dog. This is nuts."

"Sleep with your piece, Sally."

"Already got it."

"And call me if you see or hear anything, okay?"

"Roger that, Harper. You two stay safe. Tell Lydia not to worry."

"And what makes you think she'll believe me?"

Sally laughed on the other end of the line and hung up.

Harper set the phone down. "I'll make some plans tomorrow morning. Until then, I think everything is fine." He pointed to the bed. "Venom is right back at his old spot."

The Doberman was sprawled across the bed in a full extension nap position. Harper pulled off one of the blankets and laid it on the ground at the side. He instructed Venom to sleep there.

Lydia hung up her towel while Harper disposed of his shorts. He set away his SIG. They crawled into the messy covers, pulling them up under their chins. As he began to fondle her under the blanket, which wasn't an unpleasant beginning, Venom jumped up on the bed and nestled down between them and farted.

"Oh wow, Venom. You eating raccoons again?" Harper asked the dog.

Venom kept his stoic stare back at his master, looking embarrassed.

CHAPTER 4

L YDIA WOKE UP in the morning to the smell of fresh coffee and the muffled sounds of Harper on the telephone in the living room below. She slipped on her robe, cinched it about her waist, and glided downstairs to join him.

She listened as he finished up a call. Noticing he had an overnight bag filled with soft items, since he never carried firearms in that bag, she looked from the bag up to his face. When they made eye contact, he nodded his head and held up his finger as if to say "just a moment."

"Okay then. I'll see you about noon. I'm on my way in about thirty, give or take. I gotta wait for a couple of my guys."

He disconnected the phone and came over to her.

She was stiff when he tried to hug her, arching her back and resisting him. "Harper, you just got back! What the heck are you doing?"

"This is nothing to do with last night. I've been called back to D.C. for a briefing, a special briefing. I don't know exactly what is it's about, but the admiral's called me back. I should only be a day, because it's just one meeting, but just in case, I brought some clothes for overnight. And I've got a couple of guys coming over to stay here. They have a van, a self-contained Sprinter van, so they can sleep out there if you want, but—"

"Well, I suppose if I can live without you, I could allow them to sleep in the house. But you didn't discuss any of that with me."

"Lydia, you know that when the admiral or the president calls, I have to go. Right?"

"But you should be here with me, Harper. After what happened last night, you can't leave me alone. I mean, where are you priorities?"

He reached out to her, but she wasn't having any of it.

"No, this is wrong. All wrong. I could be in danger here."

"Venom is here. They know that now. They aren't just going to break in and enter, Lydia."

"Says the man who was never a hostage, nearly killed, taken captive, had his memory erased, and woke up in the company of strangers who turned out to be terrorists!"

"Lydia, come on, Sweetheart. You'll have two of my men here. You'll have Venom. Sally will defend this driveway like she is guarding the gates of Heaven. I'm going to change the codes on my way down, and I'll text them to you and the guys and Sally. Not much more I can do at this point, and it's only a day. They would not have called if it wasn't important."

"Did you tell them we had an intruder?"

"No, I—"

"There you go. You're being too casual with my safety. I'm scared to death. And while the guys might be good guards, I don't know them. You even said you might have a mole in your group. What if one of them is the mole?"

"No, they aren't in my group. They're former teammates. They know what I do, and they know all about you—"

"Oh, great. So my life story is all over your little cadre of SEAL buddies. You talk about me over beers?"

"Lydia, what's gotten into you?" He walked silently over to her and propped her chin up with his thumb and forefinger. "Sweetheart, have a little more faith in me, will you? These guys would lay down their lives for you. So would Venom. For that matter, so would Sally. You're surrounded by people who love you. Three people who love you, four counting Venom. You're about as safe as you can be."

"But you're not here."

"Just for twenty-four hours. Maybe a little longer. You're just getting yourself all upset. Don't let the fear win. I understand it, because I feel the same way. But it doesn't take me out of the picture so I can think straight. You can't afford to go into that mode; you have to stay strong."

He was right, of course, which infuriated her.

"One day. That's all. Twenty-four hours. If you're not home in twenty-four hours, I'm going to beat you up something silly," she said.

Harper got a sparkle in his eye. "I'm kinda looking forward to that. Would you do it naked? Or maybe wear some of those—?"

She picked up a pillow from the couch and threw it at him.

They heard tire tracks on the driveway. Harper checked the window. "That's them."

He opened the door, and two fit and handsome gentlemen about ten years younger than Harper stepped inside. They shook Harper's hand but immediately came over to Lydia, paying her the most deference.

"We're here to keep you safe, ma'am. You have nothing to worry about. You just sleep, go about your day, and we'll take care of everything else. Promise. I'm Danny, and this here is my former Teammate Greg,

Greg Fowler."

"Nice to meet you both."

Harper stood next to them, his arm around Danny. "We all served on Kyle's Team 3 together years ago, before I met you. They live here in Sonoma County. Danny here works with Nick and Devon over at—"

"Harper, I don't remember them. You keep forgetting that."

She could see he'd been embarrassed by her comment. He was anxious to go. He turned to the men. "Well, gents, you have your work cut out for you. I've got to fly."

He grabbed her so quickly she didn't have time to object. "Gonna miss you terrible, Lydia. You'll see. This will all be a piece of cake, but I'm glad we're taking precautions anyway."

She allowed herself to soften and gave him a long kiss on the lips, brushing her fingers over the right side of his face. "You come back in one piece. I'll do the same. Hope it's successful, whatever it is."

"Yes, ma'am. Or I'll be looking forward to that beating you told me about earlier."

Lydia felt her cheeks blush. Both the newcomers bowed their head as if they didn't see but chuckled.

She walked with Harper out to his truck. "I'm sorry I gave you a hard time. You didn't deserve that."

He walked back to her. "Honey, you've been

through a lot. Hell, I'm just lucky you allow me to jump your bones. Like you said, I'm a complete stranger. I appreciate you giving us another chance."

She decided to be snarky, wondering if it was the right option.

"Well, at least the sex is pretty fuckin' fantastic!"

He picked her up and swung her around, making her giggle. "I love it when you talk dirty. Now I'm going to have a hard-on all the way to D.C.."

Still embraced in his arms, she shed a tear as he pulled away and waved, getting into the cab. He didn't look back as he turned around and drove away. Venom had come outside, sat, and leaned against her.

"You're going to miss him too. I distracted him. He would have said goodbye if I hadn't done that. You know he loves you. I'll take care of you, okay?"

The dog looked up at her with love in his eyes. She nuzzled him nose-to-nose.

Once inside, she gave room directions. While she was showing them the kitchen, refrigerator, and the coffee maker, all of their phones buzzed. It was Harper giving them the new gate codes.

"Okay, well, I guess we're secure. You need any-thing before I go upstairs and get dressed? You each have your own bathroom. But I have extra toiletries if you need it."

"I'd just like a big glass of water. I'll get it if you just point the way," said Danny Bizbee. Greg agreed.

She pulled out two tall tumblers. "Ice?"

"Please."

Lydia filled them with crushed ice and then water and handed them off. "Feel free to make something for your breakfast, if you want. I'm going to go upstairs. I might try to catch a few more z's first, if you don't mind."

"No problem. You expecting any visitors? Deliveries? Anything we should know about? Do you have workmen coming over?"

"Harper doesn't let anyone on the property. He does it all himself. We have a drop box downtown for deliveries, so none of them. But I should tell you about something that happened to me yesterday."

"Should we sit?" asked Greg.

Lydia took the loveseat. Venom sat next to her. "Oh, and this is Venom."

"We've met Venom before. While you were gone. We've been here a lot over the past two years."

"I'll bet. Watching over Harper. Sally told me how bad it was."

"We don't leave a man behind, ma'am. Just because we don't serve together, we're still a Brotherhood."

"I get it. So you guys have families?"

"I got family but divorced, unfortunately. They live down in San Diego. My ex married another SEAL, so…"

"That's crappy."

"Not if you knew his ex," said Danny, and then everyone laughed.

"It's hard on the ladies, isn't it?" she asked them.

"When we're in, they feel nothing is more important than their team. That's not really true, but if we aren't careful, the family gets to feeling like their second best. Everyone knows their dad or husband is a war hero. Nobody wants to talk to the wife or kids. It's not fair. I'm here to tell you, though, we don't really feel that way at all. I think in my case, I just didn't know how to talk to Alex. I wasn't very good at lifting her up when she was hurt. But I loved her, love her still. She's better off," said Greg. "He's a fine man, and he's good with the kids. I get them every time I want. They're getting to the age where their activities are so demanding, hard for me to be a part of it, living up here. So we'll see. I may want to relocate. But it sure is nice up here. We got a good community I trust. San Diego's a little crazy."

"I agree with you," she said. "Wait a minute, I don't remember living down there—Oh my gosh! I just remembered a little house a couple of blocks… Oh, I wish Harper was here so I could tell him. I remember something!"

"That's wonderful," said Danny. "Go ahead and

talk. Maybe more things will come out."

She covered her face with her hand. "With my memories gone, I have to say we're falling in love all over again. I try not to compare myself to the old me—the one I can't remember. But I'm asking him all the time."

She started to blush again.

"So you guys are on your honeymoon. Best time of my life," said Greg. "I'll never forget those days, and nights!"

They all laughed again.

"You had something you wanted to tell us?" asked Danny.

"Did he tell you we had an intruder last night?"

"Oh, yes," Danny added. "Sure did. That's why we're here, ma'am."

"Please, stop with the 'ma'am.' Okay?"

They both answered, "Yes, ma'am."

"Old habits. What do you want to be called?"

"Lydia, just Lydia!"

"Fair enough, Lydia," answered Danny. "Your wish is my command."

"So what about you? Are you married?"

"Not yet. Haven't found the right one yet. I'm doing lots of testing." He grinned. "I've been dangerously close, but the guys talked me out of it." He turned to Greg, who punched him in the arm.

"I was hot and heavy for his ex's twin. Almost became brothers-in-law."

"Oh, wow. I'm sorry."

"Things have a way of working out the right way, don't they? You believe in that, Lydia?"

"I do. And if they don't, you have this thing in your brain where it shuts off and you can't remember a thing."

Nobody laughed this time.

"What was it that happened yesterday?" Danny asked again.

"I saw a couple in the Sprouts market. Not sure why, but they caught my attention. I felt like they were following me around. Had a baby carrier strapped to the top of the cart, but the blankets didn't look like they were wrapped around a baby. I thought maybe it was a small dog or something. But nothing moved. It was just so odd. It was a baby carrier, the blankets were wrapped like you'd wrap an infant, but I couldn't see a face. And then I'd bump into them later in the store. It just gave me the chills."

"You must have sensed something. Are you gifted like that?" Greg asked.

"I think so, but don't remember. Anyway, I wanted to exit the store so I could take a picture of their car and the plates for Harper to check. They disappeared. Later, on the way home, I stopped at the nursery to look at some plants, and I brought Venom inside this time. He alerted to a car in the parking lot, and the man came walking right through the office, into the back garden area where we were. Venom gave him a little scare. And just like that, he left. I didn't see him following me home. But last night around midnight, Venom alerted to something downstairs, and he barked, just wouldn't quit. He'd sensed something, and I saw our gate swing closed as Venom tried to chase them. I just have this sinking feeling they were here just to let us know they were here, know what I mean?"

The two looked at each other and nodded.

"Harper didn't seem to be too concerned about it. But then, he does that."

"Oh yeah, we're familiar with that one too," said Greg.

"When the admiral calls, he goes. That brings you guys over here. I don't have to tell you that if Venom alerts, pay attention. He's got that guy's scent imprinted now."

"You wouldn't think they'd want to mess with you. Why? If they knew you had the dog, why take the risk? It doesn't make sense. Maybe that's what Harper was thinking," answered Danny.

"Just to be sure, I'm staying home today. If Harper stays over in D.C., will you guys be able to stay here too?"

"Yes, ma'am—er—Lydia. Sorry," said Danny.

"I've got some gardening to do. Maybe you can help me with that."

"Glad to help. Just say the word," said Greg.

Lydia decided she liked these two. Her comfort level was returning. It would still be better with Harper at her side, but she had Venom and the boys. And she knew Sally could blow up the whole mountain if she needed her. It wouldn't be long. Harper would be back.

She welcomed a return to normal. But it was hard to shake the feeling something terrible was about to happen, and there wasn't anything she could do to stop it.

CHAPTER 5

T HE DAY WENT by quickly. Both Danny and Greg helped move plants and weed, as well as hauled some topsoil for the new planting that Lydia did. She had added several flats of snapdragons and impatiens she bought at the nursery two days before.

Venom wandered through the greenery of the garden, exploring holes and dirt caves the squirrels made, sniffing butterflies and flowers that waved in the gentle breeze of the Spring day. Occasionally, he came over to investigate what Lydia was planting, getting in the way until she could pet him, sometimes knocking her over in the process.

He needed to be a part of everything she did. Soon, he transferred that interest to the soil Greg and Danny were depositing into the garden from the compost and mushroom manure pile down by the large garden shed. He sometimes stopped their forward momentum, getting in the way of the wheelbarrow or getting too close to the holes they were digging and had to be lovingly pushed aside, of course, after a pet and some nice attention.

Lydia laughed when she saw this. He didn't want anyone to take him for granted or forget he was part of the process. It was a Doberman trait.

At the end of their garden work, they picked tender baby zucchini, fresh green beans, and some tomatoes for salad and vegetables for dinner. Lydia asked them if they had met Sally, their neighbor, and both men said they remembered her from previous visits.

"I think I'll invite her to dinner if you don't mind. I know Venom misses her when he doesn't see her more than once a week."

"That's fine with us. She's a quirky, fun lady," said Danny.

Sally was delighted with the invitation, and close to six o'clock, she arrived, bringing some fresh baked bread, which was a hit with Danny and Greg. Lydia made sure they had a full quarter pound of butter to go along with it.

They consumed the steaks she had bought for Harper's return, dividing them up into four pieces, which was plenty. The green beans and garden salad were a hit also. As with any good meal, there were no leftovers.

She did have blackberry pie Harper had never got

to eat when they were so occupied in the bedroom, and when she brought this out, her place amongst the cooking goddesses of the universe was secure.

"I'd ask you to marry me, but you're already taken!" joked Danny. "But promise, anything happens to Harper—"

Lydia gave him a sharp look.

"You'll not talk like that here. I've just fed you, for Chrissakes, Danny. Not nice."

"I didn't mean it—"

She cut him off. "I don't care what you meant. Don't say that around me. Ever."

"Yes, ma'am," he said sheepishly. "Very sorry. I should have thought."

"No," Sally began, "You were not thinking. You were eating. Men don't think when they eat," she continued. "But that's a forgivable offense, in my world."

Their meal was also accompanied by Coppola and Bone Frog Vineyards wines from Healdsburg. Bone Frog Vineyards was also run by former teammates, Lydia explained to the audience who already knew this.

"I apologize if I am sharp about Harper and his safety. With all this stuff going on, I'm having a hard time coping—" She stopped as tears flashed down her cheeks.

"Never mind, Lydia," said Sally, with her arm

around her shoulder. "You cry all you want. Nobody thinks anything will happen to Harper. You're not used to him being gone and then back a day and then gone again. Right, boys?" she asked them.

"We talked about it earlier. It's the hardest part of being the support person. The not knowing is hardest. Making decisions at the home front without having both parties to consult. It's tough."

"It's why we always say the whole family serves," added Greg.

Lydia made coffee, and over pie, Sally told some of her stories working in the court system, dealing with families in crisis.

"You going to retire someday, Sally?" Lydia asked.

"Well, as you can see, I don't have much of a life outside you guys and my work. It's what I do. No, they'll have to shove me off a cliff to get me to quit."

"Mr. Right hasn't appeared yet?" Danny asked.

Everyone called foul. Lydia was the first to speak.

"Danny, for a handsome, savvy guy with mad killer skills and unbelievable strength, you sure have a lack of common sense," she shouted at him, pointing to him with her fork.

"Don't," Sally continued. "I'm not—"

"Well, I am."

"What did I say?" asked Danny.

"If you haven't figured it out yet, Danny, and I

don't know for sure, but just based on her conversation, you think she'd want a man around the house? Come on. Have a brain."

Sally was embarrassed.

"I didn't say I didn't want a man around. I don't understand them. And, based on what I see every day, I'm not sure I would. No, Harper's the closest thing to a man friend I want. And Venom."

Venom perked his ears and came over to her. "Yes, we understand each other, don't we?" she said as she nuzzled his ears and petted his head.

The dog sat and worshiped Sally with his stare.

"Can I feed him a little bit of steak?" she asked.

"Sure. He's not allowed to eat away from his bowl, but I can see he'd appreciate it."

Sally was full of more stories, and then she talked about the intruder they had the night before and her decision to find a dog to adopt.

"I've done some calling around, and there are some no-kill shelters I'd like to support. I've got an appointment to go down and see a couple of them tomorrow. What do you think about getting a rescue Doberman?" she asked Lydia and the group.

"Depends on how they've been raised," said Danny. "I think they're very reliable, like any dog, but if they've been abused, they're gonna have issues. I've never known anybody to rescue a Doberman who wasn't happy, though. They adjust. And they want to please so badly that they'll usually retrain easily. Only thing you have to understand is, if they've been beaten, they're going to need a lot of care so you've got to ask yourself if you can commit to that."

"And they want me to sign something that says I'll take a disabled dog," Sally said.

"If it's just medication, that shouldn't be too bad," added Lydia.

Greg popped up. "Depends on the medication. Some of it can be pretty expensive. But I hear you, and it's a shame a good dog might not get adopted because of that. I think the main factor is you just have to see if you bond with the dog. That's the most important. All the rest, just comes along with the dog. And they'll love you for it."

"And as a breed, well, we always use the Belgians, but they can be really hard to handle sometimes. And I think a Doberman would be perfect for you, Sally," Greg said. "Most loyal dog out there."

"Well, that settles it then. One shelter has four and are expecting a litter of puppies, I guess. I don't think I want a puppy."

They cleaned the dishes, and Lydia took Venom outside after she fed him.

The night had turned colder, more crisp. She walked with him down the driveway to let him forage for his favorite spot before they'd all retire for the evening. She headed back toward the porch and sat down on a rocking chair, watching him investigate the weeds until he found a good spot. This was his favorite place.

She checked her cell phone to see if there were any messages from Harper and didn't find any. Something caught her eye, and she saw a shadow on the driveway. Looking closer, she realized it was Venom, but he was walking with a lilt or limp of some kind. Finally, in the starlight, she saw the dog collapse on the road and moan, more like a cry out for help. It was a high-pitched sad moan.

Everything in Lydia's body went on full alert. Venom was in danger.

She ran inside and called the boys, who passed her, running, beating her to get to Venom on the roadway.

"He—he's breathing, but he's foaming at the mouth. I'd say he's been poisoned," said Greg.

"Oh my God! We have to get him to the hospital," shouted Lydia. "I don't know where to take him."

Sally caught up to the group. "You take him down to the Sonoma Valley Pet Hospital, just right near downtown. That's where he always takes Venom. They know him there. And it's an emergency hospital, so they can treat him. Let's get him down there right away. I'll make a call and let them know."

Lydia was sobbing, completely inconsolable. Danny brought a big towel from the house, and they laid Venom down in the back of Lydia's SUV. Sally agreed to stay at the house by herself while both of the men accompanied Lydia and Venom to the vet. She handed Lydia her jacket.

"Take this. You'll need it."

"Don't you want one of them to stay behind? For protection?"

"I brought my sidearm. I never go anywhere without it. I'll be fine. I may not be able to stay up all night, if it takes that long, but I'll blast the first thing that comes through any of your doors unannounced," she quipped.

Lydia found her car keys in her jacket pocket and tossed them to Danny. They took off within seconds.

Upon arrival, the vet techs had a stretcher ready to take him inside for an emergency look. The dog was breathing heavily, blood starting to come from his nose and mouth, which alarmed Lydia to no end. She hadn't stopped crying since they found him in the driveway.

"We'll take him inside. I'll get some x-rays right away, and we'll get some bloodwork. What do you think it is?" the technician asked.

"We think he's been poisoned. We've had some trouble with intruders. That's all I can guess. He was fine until he went out to do his business, and then I think he ate something, but I don't know. He's been with us all day inside. When he was in the backyard, we've been with him the whole time," Lydia said.

"First, we're going to pump his stomach if there's no obstruction. We'll get back to you as soon as we can."

"You have an emergency doctor here now right?" she asked.

"Yes, he's just finishing up a patient, but he'll be right in. Don't worry. We're gonna get on it right now."

Lydia dumped herself in one of the chairs in the waiting room. She got out her phone but hesitated to leave a message for Harper. At the last minute, she changed her mind several times and then sent him a text.

"Venom has been poisoned, I'm guessing. At the vets now. Call me when you can."

Both men were very consoling for her. Danny assured her, since they caught it so early, less than a half an hour from discovery to getting him at the vet, that they'd seen cases like this where the dogs survived. But not knowing what he had taken, of course, things could act a lot faster.

There wasn't anything they could tell her that would make her feel better. She got up and began to pace back and forth. Danny brought all of them a cold bottle of water from the front desk. She wasn't concerned about price or how long it would take, whatever Venom needed, she would provide. Nothing else mattered; she couldn't let Venom die.

It was nearly forty-five minutes later when the veterinarian came out to the lobby. He had a splash of blood on his apron, which concerned Lydia and made her knees wobble. She grabbed on to Greg's sleeve as she stood and braced herself for the news.

"Well, we've done what we can. We pumped his stomach. For sure, it was poison, but we don't think he ingested much of it. His stomach contents had a white powdery substance, and it must have been bitter to discourage him from eating it. From your description of his behavior after ingestion and what we saw during intake, the effects seem to primarily be neurological. While we can't test exactly what it came from here, we can send the stomach contents off for evaluation, or you might want to check the area Venom was in to see if you can find additional samples to send out. Our lab can do an analysis if you want."

He shook his head sadly. "I'm not sure if there is permanent damage to his organs or neurological system yet, but we did baseline bloodwork, which looks normal. We have him on IV fluids to support his kidneys as they process the poison. I also have him lightly sedated and on oxygen, because breathing has been difficult for him. This should give him some time to let his body recover. His gums and lips are turning back pink, did that almost immediately after we pumped his stomach, so that's a good sign."

She was relieved. "Will there be long-term effects?"

"It's too soon to tell. We'll monitor him closely. Do you put out rat poison? Or does he eat dead animals that might have ingested rat poison secondhand? Or do you have a neighbor you are quarreling with who might take it out on him?"

"Harper always jokes about him eating dead raccoons."

"Sometimes dogs can eat squirrels or rabbits that died of poison and get a dose that way. But we didn't see any evidence of it in his stomach," he said.

"No, Venom is very disciplined. He's not supposed to eat things not in his bowl. And he's been trained that way. He was only gone for like thirty seconds. Didn't take the time to go check the field but will do that when we get home. Do you need a sample of that before you can determine what else to do?"

"We're going to monitor him overnight, and with him sedated, being in the room might cause him to fight the medication. So I would say go home and look for some evidence. It appears it may have been laced raw hamburger meat, judging by the appearance of the contents. If that isn't his normal supper, I would guess it was poisoned meat. And meat, especially raw meat, it's pretty hard for a dog to avoid."

They agreed to leave him at the hospital. Lydia wanted to see him before she left, so the vet showed her back to the recovery room. He was in a large kennel lying down on a soft blanket. He had IVs in his right leg and seemed to be sleeping soundly. He still had a light red bloody ooze from his mouth and nose, but not nearly as deep red as it had been before.

"What causes the blood?" she asked the vet.

"It's bleeding, stomach lining bleeding. We'll probably send him home with sucralfate and a week's worth of prescription diet that is formulated to be easy on the stomach while it heals. We've given him some antibiotics in case it is something that carries infection. Just as a precaution."

Lydia reached her hand through the bars but couldn't touch Venom, so the vet opened the door and allowed her to speak to him and pet his head and the length of his body. He was sweating but otherwise seemed to be calm.

"I'm here. We're here for you. We're gonna make you all better. You just try your best to get well, okay? We're not leaving you. We're all here. Love you, Venom."

Danny put his arm around her as she sniffled her way from the emergency room back to the lobby and then out to her car. Greg drove while Lydia sat in the backseat by herself, silently weeping.

Of all the things that could happen—and she'd warned Harper about this—all of the things she predicted had come true. Harper was satisfied that Venom was an adequate deterrent to anybody who would want to mess with them. But it turned out Venom could be compromised, and she felt guilty she hadn't been more careful watching him. She'd had that premonition that something was going to happen.

She thought about whether or not she'd seen anybody on the driveway as they came up the road and punched in the new code for the lower gate. It opened quickly. And then closed behind them as they drove on their way to the second gate. They passed Sally's house, her lights were still on. Her car was gone, since it was up at Lydia and Harper's.

They punched in the code for the second gate and drove up, seeing the sprinter van and Sally's Jeep park next to it. She was relieved.

"Did you guys text her? I sure don't want to come through the front door and get blasted in my own house."

"All taken care of, Lydia," said Danny, holding up his phone.

The front door was locked, but after a few seconds, Sally opened the door and looked with anticipation at her. She was worried.

"He's stable for now. They put him into an induced coma. They figured that it's poison."

Sally grabbed her in her arms, "Oh my dear, I'm so sorry. I'm just so sorry. Did you tell Harper?"

"I tried to. I left him a message."

"Greg and I are going to go down and search the brush and see if we can find what he ate. Do you have a couple baggies or a container of some kind in case we find it?" said Danny.

"Yes, let me get you some." She tore from her embrace with Sally, ran to the kitchen, and grabbed a handful of baggies. "These work?"

The two of them took off with flashlights.

Sally directed her to sit down on the couch and offered to get her some tea or a glass of water. Lydia said she'd have a little bit of tea with her if she didn't mind making it.

Sally shouted from the kitchen. "Whoever this is, Lydia, it's really something I think you need to tell the police about. I know Harper will have a way he wants to do this, but you've got to get law enforcement involved. They will do the investigation. Maybe there's a string of these going on."

"You mean, not the same people that came by the other night? Not the weird couple at the store? It's just all coincidence? It's too weird to be an isolated incident. I think they are all related, Sally."

"I wish I could tell you I didn't believe that, but I think you're right. And we need some direction from Harper. Why don't you try calling him again?"

"I'll do it in a minute. Let me see what they find outside first. He's gotten the text, and usually, he reads his texts and doesn't listen to voicemail. But something must be going on. He's out of communication."

The men came inside with several baggies of small bits of what look like red hamburger meat and raw steak. "We found several places with the stuff. I can't tell which he ate from, but there's about ten balls of it planted everywhere out in the field. It's obvious they intended to get him. This was directed toward Venom, not toward you or anybody else. They wanted to get Venom out of the picture," said Danny.

"Should I call the police?" Lydia asked.

"What about Harper? What does he say?" Greg asked.

"I haven't talked to him yet. I hope he'll get back to me soon. If he agrees, we need to report this. But I'll wait for Harper."

Greg asked her another question. "Did you see anybody out there, like was the gate open or could you tell if there was a car? Did you hear anything, Lydia?"

"No. Somebody could've walked up the driveway, but it's a mile and a half long. It's not an easy walk, but if they couldn't get in because we changed the codes, they could walk around it. The gate just goes across the driveway, but the area isn't fully fenced until up top."

"Unless they came from the park next door," suggested Sally. "You know there's a regional trail that goes right by your property line. It's not more than a quarter-acre away, few hundred yards. Somebody could go to the regional park and climb over the cattle fence—it's barbwire, but if they cut it, they could do it. They could make it up to your place and then back out without the use of a vehicle."

It seemed the most logical choice.

An hour went by and still no call from the vet. They had promised an update by that time. So Lydia called them.

"Hi. This is Lydia Cunningham. I'm calling about Venom."

"Mrs. Cunningham, the doctor will give you a call soon. We're still working with him. He's not finished. I'm sorry it's taken so long, but we've had some things come up. The doctor will tell you everything."

Lydia dropped the phone and sank into her lap, crying.

Sally picked her phone up "I'm sorry. She's pretty upset. Is he still alive?"

Lydia held her breath. It was a question she hadn't wanted to ask.

"Oh yes. It's just that the doctor is involved in a couple other emergencies, so he hasn't had a chance to call, but he will. Yes, Venom's still sleeping."

"Oh, that's good. Thank you." She hung up the phone and placed it on the coffee table in front of Lydia. She came around and sat next to her.

"My dear, that dog is an angel. I just don't think there's any way in hell God would part you guys from that beautiful animal. Have faith, Lydia, trust me. Somehow, we'll get to the bottom of this, and Venom will have his revenge. I swear."

CHAPTER 6

S ALLY WAS ESCORTED back to her house by Danny, after refusing Lydia's generous offer to put her up at her house overnight.

"No, I've been living alone too long, Lydia. Thanks, but I'm fine by myself. If the gods out there decide this should be the night that somebody wants to do me in, so be it. I've had a long and fruitful life. For sure though, I'll take a big chunk out of them first."

Everyone laughed with her fearless attitude. But Lydia was still worried for her safety.

Danny came back from Sally's and told Lydia he was impressed with her massive art collection and antiques. "She's kind of a pack rat, but she does have some nice things there. Nice lady. I'm sorry I offended her. And I apologized."

"I'll bet she turned it down again, right?" said Lydia.

"Oh yeah, she gave me a piece of her mind. Boxed

my ears a bit. Scolded me for not thinking. I agreed with her and apologized again. She told me to quit doing that. Demanded it, in fact."

"I'll bet you learned your lesson," said Greg.

"I never do, but it was a good wake-up call. So what's up? Any news?"

"You mean in the ten minutes you've been gone?" Lydia answered.

"Just trying to be helpful."

"No, nothing. It's going to be a while, I think. I'm a little surprised Harper hasn't called, but it's usually for good reason. I'm not gonna try them again. It must be important."

At just that moment, the Sonoma Valley Pet hospital called.

"Hello?" she said in anticipation.

"Hi, Lydia. This is Dr. Gordon. I'm calling to give you an update on Venom. His vitals are stable. We are still slightly concerned about his breathing, though that has also improved slightly. I'm going to keep him under sedation and on oxygen, with your blessing, of course. We'll continue to give him fluids, and we'll run bloodwork again periodically to make sure nothing has changed since admittance. Typically, we recommend a minimum of two days on fluids with monitoring after poison ingestion, but if his respirations stabilize and he seems calm, we'll likely wake him up tomorrow."

"Do whatever's best, Dr. Gordon. That's great news."

"He's a strong dog and a very good boy too, from what I understand. I remember treating him in the past. While prognosis is always guarded, I'm hopeful he's going to pull through. Are you on board with the plan?"

"Dr. Gordon, we've had sort of an event here. Harper is gone for a day, and we're hoping he should be back tomorrow. But Venom is sort of my guard dog. I know he can't do that now, obviously, but we feel the poisoning has been intentional, and we're looking to bring the police in. He's probably safer down there," she answered.

"That sounds good, Mrs. Cunningham. I'll keep him here, and if there's any change, good or bad, I'll give you a call. I think it's more important right now that you get some rest. And if Mr. Cunningham calls, I'll make sure the staff knows to wake me up. I'm gonna be spending the night down here. We had a whole lot of emergencies this weekend, so I'm pretty tied up. Don't think I'm gonna be making it home for one or two days. But you rest and take care of yourself and be safe, okay? And I've saved some of the material from the stomach. Have you found the items he may have ingested?"

"Yes, we have what looks like hamburger meat, and

my guys here say there were at least ten spread out throughout the field, and they've got them all tucked in separate baggies. I am sure we could bring one down to you to send out for testing."

"It wouldn't hurt. We retained several samples from his stomach, and we'll just see what the concentration level is. If there's any variety in the baggies, that would also tell us what group he got it from. Sometimes, these things are different if someone made the cocktail in their kitchen, whether a strong dose or not a strong dose. It might help. In either case, it would be evidence for the police, should you go that far. So you bring it down when you can. Like I said, I'll be here all night."

"I'll have Danny bring it right down to you. Thanks so much, doctor, for giving us a call."

"No problem."

She disconnected the phone and grinned at her two companions. "I'm so happy, and I'm so glad I got this news before I had to break it to Harper. I'm gonna try to call him again. Danny, would you mind running a few of the bags down to the doctor?"

"On it. Do you want me to take your car again or the van?"

"No, you can take my car."

He held up the keys, showing that he still had them.

Greg joined her in the living room, bringing her a

glass of water.

"Thanks. Now if I can just get a hold of Harper…"

"What's the meeting about?"

"I'm not sure. But you know about this new team he's on? Are you going to be joining?"

"I haven't been asked yet. I think he was going to, but not officially. He did ask Danny. I suppose he thinks it would get over to me. I'll probably get the call, but I'm not sure I want to do it. Like I said, I might want to move back to San Diego and be closer to the kids. Whole reason for getting out of the teams was to be closer to the family, and then I moved up here." He shrugged.

"But you get to work with friends, right?"

"That's part of it. I might be ready now."

"Maybe it's time. You'll be able to have a better chance at a fresh start down there. I hope so."

Lydia dialed Harper's number, who picked up on the first ring.

"Lydia? Lydia? Are you okay? How's Venom? I got your message. What's the prognosis?"

"Looks like he's going to be okay, Harper. Oh, so good to hear your voice. I was—"

"Tell me about Venom?"

"Well, we took him into the emergency room. Dr. Gordon said he'd eaten some poisoned pieces of meat. And he asked us to go search in the field, so Danny and

Greg went out there and walked through the area carefully. They picked up ten little baggies of hamburger meat. We think it was laced with something, some poison. Danny's bringing them down to the doctor right now for an analysis. They pumped his stomach, saved some of the contents, and put him into a coma for overnight to see how his other organs hold out. Doesn't appear he has any stoppage or didn't eat something that blocked his insides at all, which a lot of poisons do. His stomach had meat remnants and brown fluid. It may have scarred some of his stomach lining, because he was coughing up and snorting blood. It wasn't very pretty. But I think we got it in time. And the doctor just told me that he thinks he'll be fine without any problems. But he has to get through this night first."

"Thank God. I didn't even think that somebody would resort to that."

"Yeah, when we plan and do our best, like you always told me, enemy gets a vote."

Harper paused. "You know, Lydia, I don't think I've told you that since you've been back. I think that's something you heard from me from before. Are your memories coming back?"

"I had something else that happened today I'll tell you about when you get back. But I think little spots are coming back here and there. I can't be sure. Anyway, the boys have been great, and it'll be wonderful to have you back home. Do you have to leave again for a while?"

"I need to talk to you about a couple of things first. It's a possibility you're gonna have to come back here."

"To D.C.? Now? Whatever for?"

"No, not now. In the future. I'm waiting on some instructions. I don't want to talk about it over the phone, so let me do it when I get home, Sweetheart. That's great news, and I'm gonna crash now, and then I'll be home as soon as I can. It's later here than it is down there, so give me a break, okay?"

"Done deal."

She sat the phone down. She was going to be able to see him at last!

Danny returned and informed them that the dog was still improving, staying sedated but vital signs were getting stronger.

"They were quite happy to get the samples. There's one that looks like it has some kind of purplish chalk stuff in the middle of it. I've seen stuff like that. That's a sign of strychnine."

"Yeah, I've seen it too. You know the sheep ranches out at the coast, on Coleman Valley Road? They have a big problem with coyotes, keeping them away from the sheep, especially the spring lambs. They put tires on the fence, and they put the poison inside the tires so that other animals can't get it, but the coyotes will find it and sniff it out. It's an effective way to poison them. It would've been easy for somebody to just pick up some of that stuff, since I don't think it's under lock and key anywhere," said Greg.

"You're right about that. I remember seeing that too," said Lydia. This was also something from the past. Even though she didn't like the circumstances, she was hopeful that a few pieces of the puzzle were beginning to form.

"What else did Harper say?" asked Greg.

"He said I might have to go back to D.C.. I can't imagine why."

"Something to do with your kidnapping?" asked Danny.

"Maybe, I don't know. I just know that the guy ratted on a whole bunch of people, including his parents. Apparently, he's gonna be locked away for a long time. I'm just not sure what they need from me as far as testimony or statement, but maybe it's something completely different."

"Just the same, it's kind of cool to get an audience with the president or the admiral, if that's what it is," Danny added.

"As long as Harper's there and Venom too, I'm okay."

CHAPTER 7

LYDIA RECEIVED WORD that Harper would be returning before noon. The sleek black executive car pulled up the driveway, and she waved to the driver. Harper brought his overnight bag and a briefcase with him as he extricated his huge frame out of the backseat. He dropped them as soon as he saw Lydia and ran to her giving her a big hug and kiss.

His arms around her gave her new life. She hadn't realized how exhausted she'd been.

"How are you doing, Sweetheart?" he whispered. "Everything okay here?"

"I'm just so glad you're home. I may not ever let you leave the house again," she said through tears. He lifted her chin up with his thumb and forefinger and gave her a warm kiss.

"You're a lot stronger than that, Lydia. I've got some things we need to go over, and thank God Venom is going to be okay, but never doubt I'll be here to save you. We're all here to keep you safe. Just keep trusting, believing that will happen, okay? We both have to be strong right now."

"I will. It's just a one-two punch with all the uncertainty of what's going on. It gets to me, Harper. I think it's because of, you know, all the stuff that went on before. I'm getting worn out."

"I get it. But if you're going to doubt something, doubt that fact. You're way stronger than anyone thinks you are, except me. I need you now to get that strength back. And you have plenty to be agitated about, but, Lydia, just remember, we don't think straight when we're worried or upset about things. Especially worry. It does no good. Most cases we can't do anything about the things we're worried about anyway. And half of them aren't true. Thank goodness Venom's in good hands and he'll be home soon. And you've got two great protectors here who I know took very good care of you."

"They were amazing. Really amazing. I agree."

"And they'll be back again just as soon as we need them. So you hang on. Let me say hi to the guys, and then you and I have to sit down and have a talk, okay?"

She bit her lower lip and allowed him to pass her by. He gave a shake and hug to both his men. She couldn't hear what they were saying, little whispers here and there, but it was lighthearted and jovial. And they had been such good companions. She would not have been able to stand the twenty-four hours with him being gone without them. And Sally, she would remember to tell Harper about Sally.

He put his arm around her and led her into the house.

"Harper and Lydia, we're going to go downtown and grab a little bite to eat, kind of check in on our to-do lists, if you don't mind. We'll be back in an hour and a half, is that okay?" Danny asked.

"You don't have to come back if you don't want to. I think everything's okay. I'll catch up with you by phone tomorrow."

"Well, you just let us know if you need us back."

"You need to pack?"

"Nope, we're all set to go," he answered.

"Hey, Boss, you sure?" asked Greg.

"Nah, we're good. I have some important things to go over with Lydia. I'd rather have the house, if you don't mind. And I'm dead tired. I'll call you if something comes up. And thanks! As they say, your debit is in the mail!"

They all laughed.

"Yes, sir," said Danny. "A pleasure."

"Oh and, Danny, don't you go too far. Got some stuff I need to talk to both of you about regarding Silver Team. Make sure you check in with me before you go anywhere far."

"Done deal, sir. Thank you." To her, Danny said, "Ma'am, it was a pleasure. And I'm sure glad we got to get reacquainted with Venom too. Best of luck with that. I know he's gonna be just fine. And you tell your neighbor, she is a kick in the pants."

"Adios," said Greg, waving. They climbed in the Sprinter van and took off down the driveway.

Lydia inhaled deeply as they walked back into their sanctuary. The first thing he commented on were the Gloriosa Daisies on the table top. "Those are lovely, Sweetheart. Just feels like home now that I've seen you and seen these. I miss Venom. Are we gonna go get him later on today or is it tomorrow?"

"They're supposed to let me know about three. There's a possibility it could be today. It depends on how well he does."

"Well, we have plenty to discuss until then. So do you want to brew me some coffee, real strong coffee? We need to sit at the dining room table. I have to show you something."

"Oh? Did you run across a problem in D.C.?" she asked while she put water on for coffee.

Harper followed her into the kitchen after setting his laptop on the dining room table. "There's been a development in the Lipori case, and one of the reasons I was called back there is Lipori is making all kinds of plea agreements and trying to negotiate himself a sweeter deal."

She turned and faced him. She could see in his eyes that he expected her to react negatively. She tried not to show her anger, but he probably knew it anyway. "Harper, how can that be?"

"It doesn't have to be, and it isn't for sure yet, but he's talking. He's talking about a lot of things. And I have a video of the interview I did with him that I need show you. I've received permission from everybody upstairs to do that. I just want to show you."

"This is not what I expected." She poured the hot water over the coffee grounds, stirred the mixture with her long-handled spoon, and placed the top on the French press. Then she covered the whole pot with a towel to keep the mixture warm.

"Coffee will be ready in five minutes." She had intended to be more cheerful, but it wasn't coming out that way. Finally, she gave up. "Tell me this isn't happening."

"It's the world we live in. Things can always happen, Lydia. Evil people do evil things. Most of the evil people are pretty dumb. However, there's a few that are so cunning and so dangerous that we have to take them seriously. And unfortunately, sometimes other people don't have the backbone or the spine we have. In this case, it's all going to pivot on you. I sincerely wish that wasn't the case. But you'll see in a moment. I need your help with it. Only you can guide me. I'm only going to do what you think we should do. I'm not gonna force you to do anything you don't want to."

"You're scaring me, Harper."

"We both should be scared, Sweetheart. The guy is as evil as I've seen. Very smart. Planning and plotting all the time. He doesn't like to lose."

"But he already did."

"It's not over until he's gone, permanently gone. I never told you that, understand? But that's the truth. I don't trust him, but I need you to hear what he's got planned. What he's thinking."

"Like what?"

"Let's watch the video first. And then we'll talk. It's not really long. It's about twenty minutes or so. And it didn't take but minutes for me to see his long game. Didn't want to, but I have to, Lydia. He let me see who he really is."

"How does this affect me?"

"He's much more dangerous than anyone gave him credit for. You are very lucky that he spared you. Because he did. And he went to great expense to heal you, medically. He's gonna explain all that. I just want you to hear it in his voice. You can tell a lot by watching him, since you spent time at his house."

Harper looked down at his feet.

"What are you not telling me?" she asked him.

"You'll see. It was very difficult for me to do this and to bring this interview back for you. I didn't want to. But after I thought about it, I realize that if I didn't involve you now, knowing his upcoming plans, it would certainly involve you later on, and I figured it was only fair. You didn't want to be left in the dark, right?"

"True."

"Well, this is your chance to get the whole Monty. So try to keep an open mind, but I want you to listen to him carefully."

"Okay."

She heard the dinger go off so pushed the plunger down and poured two coffees with cream Harper brought out from the refrigerator. They sat side by side at the dining room table. Lydia was nervous as hell as Harper opened his laptop, placed his arrow at the small box in the lower right-hand side of his desktop, and watched her as the interview began.

They were in a holding cell of some sort, very dark. There was one light in the corner, which shone on Lipori's face. She had grown to hate and dislike him after she came home, but at the time, living in Italy, she had never felt she couldn't trust him. She was aware he had saved her life, right from the very start of their relationship. But she never remembered the ambush or the fact he'd tried to murder her. It was always incredible that this happened. How could it have come to be? She had so many questions.

She could see the back of Harper's head. He was sitting erect in a metal chair right across the table from her kidnapper. Lipori was handcuffed, secured at the metal table, and probably also in ankle restraints since she heard more chains rattling in the background.

"This is the interview with Jakob Lipori, convicted terrorist." Harper named off the date, the numerals of the case number, arresting jurisdictions, things which labeled the interview properly. Then he started.

"This is Special Agent Harper Cunningham. I am conducting this interview at the request of Silver Team and U.S. Department of Justice."

Harper paused, adjusted his seat, and continued.

"Mr. Lipori, please state your name for the record."

In a very respectful manner, he answered. "Yes, sir, I am Jakob Lipori."

Jakob's face was relatively unlined, his curly brown hair framing his large brown eyes and high cheekbones. He could have been an actor trying out for a film audition, a billionaire being interviewed for his lifestyle. In any other setting, he would've been considered a handsome, attractive young man. But she knew behind those eyes, now appearing as warm as just-out-of-the-oven brownies, he was a killer. And she had escaped death only because he had the whim to save her. It had nothing to do with what she or anybody else around them had done to make it so. In his evilness, he had been merciful.

"Mr. Lipori, you wanted to see me for a particular reason, and let's just verify you and I have not really discussed the action that was taken to bring you to the United States. I was the team leader that brought you back, but you and I have not had any discussions since then, correct?"

"Not unless you believe in telepathy. I've sent you a lot of hate mail."

The smile that followed was pure evil. Lydia shuddered.

"Well, I can see how you might be a little upset with me for having caught you, but under the law, what you did was not only wrong but you caused a lot of death and destruction. You're now in the process of paying the price for that. It's not my fault. You chose to do this. So you asked for this interview, and I'm here. I'm ready to listen to whatever it is you have to say."

"Well, first of all, make sure you give my warm greetings to your wife."

He stared into the camera lens. He didn't smile; he didn't even have a sparkle in his eyes. His eyes were dead. Lydia saw the deep black pools of evil residing there. He was using the fact that Harper stared down at the man who had both shot and also saved his wife, the most important person in his life. And there wasn't a thing Harper could do about it. It was a simple fact.

"Mr. Lipori, why don't we just stop playing cat and mouse and you just get out with whatever it is you have to say."

"Alright," he said calmly. "Wish I could have a cigarette. May I?"

"Sorry, not allowed in this building."

"Very well. First of all, I want to tell you I was not there to kill Lydia. As a matter of fact, she and I worked together at the mission for several weeks before the attack. I knew there was going to be an attack, and I could've left earlier or could've left and returned during the attack, as I was committed to participate in it, but I was hoping I could protect her. I had designs to do that and take her back to Italy with me. I didn't want to be her killer. I wanted to be her rescuer, and that's what I did, in the end."

"That's a stretch."

"Hear me out. As it turned out, the mission was successful, but unfortunately, she was shot in the process. I was aiming at another schoolteacher, and at the last minute, Lydia dashed out in front of my gun. It could've been that she realized what I was going to do, because up until this time, we had been good friends. I can almost say intimate friends."

Lydia saw the muscles in the back of Harper's neck constrict. She knew it took every ounce of strength he had to not reach across the table and break Lipori's neck.

"I doubt you were intimate, but perhaps that means something different to you. She's a warm, loving person. I'm sure she was good for the mission and trying to do good for those people in Africa. Probably trying to protect her colleague. You, on the other hand, were there under false pretenses. Gaining their trust and then coming in to destroy everything they did and their lives as well. I wouldn't be so proud of that if I were you, Mr. Lipori."

"Well, you have more resources. I'm a bit constrained, but I make up for it with the element of surprise, Mr. Cunningham. Those of us who are fighting for freedom sometimes do it in a different way."

"So you were fighting for freedom, then?"

"You already have your freedom, or at least you have it for now. I think the United States is entering in a new phase where all of the freedom-loving elements from all over the world are ganging up. They're all coming here, and you're letting them in with arms wide open. You are going to witness such beautiful havoc and such confusion against this country the likes of which you've never seen. It's not just in the Middle

East or Africa or Europe. It's all over—people are coming from all over the globe, anybody who has some axe to grind. South America, China, Middle East, Africa, Germany, Russia, Ukraine, Baltic countries, everybody has terrorist cells that hate the United States. You are the great Satan. It's a global movement driven by people who have nothing more to lose."

"Just to be clear here, Lipori, I'm not the great Satan. You're saying the United States is the great Satan. I might be a little bit flattered how important you think I am, but I'm sorry, I am not the great Satan of the world. And I'm sure you didn't mean that."

"No, but you can be the messenger for me."

"I'm afraid I will not be your messenger or one for any of your ridiculous friends either. That's just not gonna happen."

"We'll see how it plays out, won't we?"

"I'm getting marginally frustrated here, and I have other places to be. Let's just get on with this interview. You tell me what you want to tell me, and if it's a request you want me to make to my superiors, I'd be happy to do so. But that's the beginning and end of any kind of cooperation I'm gonna do for you. The rest of it is totally up to you. You've already turned in your own parents. You've turned in lots of other people in your movement in Germany and Italy. I don't know what it is you think you have to speak about today. You have no legitimacy."

Lipori leaned forward on his elbows, still out of reach of Harper. "Mr. Cunningham, I saved your wife's life. You owe me."

As forward as Lipori had come, Harper lay back that much and more. He shook his head and then added, "I don't owe you a damn thing, Mr. Lipori. You attempted to take her life. I'm glad you didn't. But I don't owe you a damn thing. I didn't ask you to put a bullet in her chest to take her life away or to take her heart. You nearly destroyed her. And you don't even care."

"You misunderstand me, Mr. Cunningham. I care. She is the vehicle I need."

"Need? For what?"

"She's my get out of jail free card. You do play Monopoly, don't you, Mr. Cunningham?"

"How could that possibly be?"

"Well, I believe your household has had some recent events in the last two days, some intruders?"

Harper must have reacted, because Lipori broke out in a wide grin. His smile looked fragile, unhinged, and dirty.

"And what would you know about that?"

"I know the people who are attempting to kidnap her. Yes, Mr. Cunningham, there are designs to grab Lydia and take her back to Africa. There's a very heavy ransom on her head. Did you not know this?"

"I don't believe you. Who would want her kid-napped?"

"The culprits can make money doing it, sir. Now more than ever, we can get into your country and do anything we like. We can rape, kidnap, set bombs, and steal children—all for a price. You thought your government was for sale? No, sir, your government has put a bounty on all your heads. I don't believe your State Department tells you everything, either, do they?"

"I've only heard conjecture. News pundits. I doubt they would keep something like that from me. So let's just say I don't believe you, and go on from there."

"What if I were to tell you that, in exchange for possibly some liberties with my incarceration, I can make it possible for you people to find those individuals who were paid quite a large sum of money to kidnap her? What would you say if I could make that happen, take that threat away? And what I mean by end is you can kill them or capture or whatever. Up to you. Afterall, I saved your wife the first time. You should get to save her the second. Isn't that fair?"

CHAPTER 8

H ARPER TURNED OFF the video. Lydia was locked in a frozen stare at the screen with the little arrow pointing right, indicating the interview had been stopped for now.

Her heart pounded. She didn't understand how things could get so complicated so quickly. Her lack of memory was making it dangerous for all of them. And now her husband was embroiled in a very dark possibility. If she asked Harper, she knew he'd take this guy out. He'd willingly suffer the consequences also. Without hesitation. He was like Venom on the trail of a bad guy. If she asked him, he would violate every principle of his soul. He'd do that to protect her. She knew that.

She looked up at him. He'd been so silent. His eyes were red, tears streaming down his cheeks. It broke her heart to see this. He had the expression of a defeated man.

"I can't believe what it must've taken for you to sit on this all night last night. You probably never slept, did you?"

"No, I didn't. I really didn't want to play this for you," he admitted as he looked at her through swollen, painful eyes still overflowing with tears. "I am so sorry I did not just off this guy when I had the opportunity. Had I known any of this—"

He broke up without being able to continue.

"Harper, my love, we are in this together. This is such a tremendous burden for you to carry by yourself. It was the right thing to share it with me."

"Was it? Really? You're never gonna feel safe here any longer. I've totally failed at all this. Why didn't I see the signs? Why didn't I realize what was really going on, the danger here?"

"Because you didn't have all the information. Now I know why they wanted you to play it for me. You say it's my decision, but it really isn't. We have to do what's best for the country. I want to stay here forever. I want us to live life so peaceful and loving that we never want to leave. But that isn't the reality of the world, is it? And you didn't make that happen. The world has erupted. It's no longer the world we used to dream about when we were in high school and went to dances, double dated, went to the drive-in, went for ice cream with our friends. We don't have that any longer.

It's gone."

"I'm stubborn. I don't want it to be gone. I want everything to go back to normal."

"You mean when we ran around in our convertibles and bought Starbucks drive-through. Nothing was political. Nobody was shouting and yelling at each other here. Now it's a mess. And we've allowed it to become a mess. Harper, we've been given the opportunity to clean up part of that mess. It's an opportunity to do the right thing."

"But just what is the right thing? I honestly don't have a plan, Lydia. I'm ashamed to say it. I don't have a plan this time to save you, to save me. I just don't know."

She looked down at the screen. "It says there's about five or six minutes left. Why don't you finish it? Then we'll talk some more."

His answer was simple. He pushed down the top of his laptop. "You've seen all the important stuff. The rest of it is just window dressing. Just nothing important." He looked at her again with red eyes. "Once you see the world this way, there are some things you cannot unsee. I feel like we both lost our innocence. He's right about people coming over and doing whatever the heck they want. And we can't protect everybody, can we?"

She leaned forward and took his face in her hands,

giving him all the love she felt in her chest.

"Harper, we can try. We can save some. And that's a start. We can do that together. We have to try. Remember what you used to tell me all the time? Evil exists because good men and women do nothing in the face of it? That's never been more true than today. It always was true, but we can't sit back and do nothing. What is it you want me to do?"

He inhaled deeply and then sighed. He was exhausted. Her man was looking ten years older than she'd seen him before. The weight of trying to spread himself so thin, as if he was some kind of a Superman who could save the whole world, weight on him. Although he'd done so many good things with his time on the teams and now this new Silver Team program, which had already saved numerous people and stopped several terrorist attacks, he was focusing on what he hadn't been able to do rather than what he had done.

"We can't do it alone, Harper. We need the team. I'm part of the team now. It's nothing I wanted to do with my life, trust me, but there's no way around it, is there? It's inevitable, and despite what you said, if we don't pay attention to it, it will come back when we least expect it. It will come back roaring, stronger. We need to prepare ourselves, think about it logically like you said, and set up a plan."

He nodded his head and stared at his lap. She took

his hands in hers. "Harper, look at me."

He raised his head slowly. "Lydia, I can't hardly do that. I'm so ashamed."

"Why? You've done all you could physically do!"

"I completed the mission yes. But I didn't neutralize the threat. And those two years you were gone, I didn't investigate. Just took the word for it that you were gone. And I tried to get over that. Unsuccessfully, I might say, but I should've looked into it further. This is all my fault."

She could see he was struggling and that there was nothing more talk could accomplish tonight.

"Listen, I think we should turn in early. Let's call and see if we can pick up Venom, and then let's the three of us just go to bed, to sleep. We'kk pray for resilience and strength tomorrow. I'm sure the answers will come."

"I should get the guys to come over again."

"I think that's a good idea. And I wonder if Sally is in danger, as well."

"I thought of that. I'll see if I can get a third man."

She agreed.

"This is huge. I'm not sure if the Silver Team will be able to handle this one, because it's so personal, but I'm gonna at least get the time off to be able to handle this properly."

"They've seen this video?"

"Oh yes, the president and the admiral both. They were pretty shaken. They told me to show you. They wanted you to understand what the stakes were."

"But did they say anything to you about Silver Team not getting involved?"

"Well, it's in the charter. We're not to do personal vendettas, that sort of thing. That fancy little phrase ends with 'or the appearance of,'" he said, his fingers in air quotes. "But I think he'll allow time off and let me assemble something as long as I am able to reassure them we're able to function and I don't allow these personal things to get in the way of making good decisions or risking the program or any of my men's lives. It can be done, Lydia. I just don't know if I can manage personally. And I don't know if I can get sanctions for it."

She nodded and squeezed his hands. Then she leaned over and gave him a kiss. "You need to rest, Harper. You just need to rest. You call your guys, and I'll give the vet a call and see if we can pick up Venom. I know that would make you feel better, wouldn't it?"

"You bet. But only if it's good for him."

"I got it. I'll make sure."

So while Harper called Greg and Danny, he also was able to give Sally a heads-up. He told her he had ordered a third former SEAL Team member to come watch at her house tonight. Lydia could hear Sally squawking and arguing with Harper from clear across the room, but he insisted.

The hospital came on the line.

"Oh, yes, Mrs. Cunningham! Dr. Gordon was going to give you a call and suggest it. He's up and awake, and he's feeling much better. I think he would love to come home with you guys. There's going to be some precautionary instructions, and I wouldn't let him run around outside on his own. You'll have to walk him with a leash and keep a special eye out for him and check all his potty breaks, if you know what I mean."

"It's fine with me. Just put it all in writing with instructions. We'll be down in the next twenty minutes or so to pick him up. And thank you for all you've done for him, for all you've done for me and for Harper too. Venom means the world to us."

The guys were going to arrive while they were down at the hospital. When they walked inside the lobby, the technicians behind the desk were bright and chipper.

"We're so happy for you guys. He's such a wonderful dog. Even licked our hands when we were drawing blood. He's probably not going to want to eat till tomorrow, which is normal. Just offer him small amounts throughout the day. We're sending a few cans of the special food with you to ease his stomach back into food."

"You have the written instructions for us?" Lydia asked.

Harper was standing by the access door to the rear room, waiting for his companion, his former best friend, to come out and jump into his arms. Lydia watched him, and the technician behind the desk suddenly stopped chattering instructions to allow her that moment.

The door opened, and Venom was in Harper's arms immediately, licking his face, dancing around. Dr. Gordon was trying to handle him with the leash, but Venom wouldn't have anything to do with it. He nearly pulled the doctor over on the floor.

"Well, he's sure glad to see you. And I'm happy for that. He bounced back quicker than I thought. I want you to bring him in every day for more bloodwork, and I'd like you to collect stool samples. If you see any blood in his urine or if he starts to jaundice, we want to know about it. Right now, he's clear. We flushed a lot of saline through him. No free ranging on your property for a while in case there's more poison laid out there. I think you should walk him on the leash, which is certainly more exercise than he's had here, so he should be happy with that."

As if Venom knew the doctor was talking about him, he came over and jumped to put a paw on his knee.

"You're something else, Venom. I don't think I've ever seen a Doberman like you before. Thank goodness you're still with us. You've got a lot of work to do keeping track of these two, protecting them, right?"

Venom cocked his head, as if he understood, and stared up at him. When he heard Lydia speaking to the technician behind the desk, he was over at her side, sitting, looking up at her until she bent down and pressed her forehead to his. He licked her ears, her neck. He placed his paws on her shoulder and tried to stand up, bracing himself on her upper torso. She hugged him and told him all kinds of little things that he liked to hear. He was squealing, almost a painful moan, but delighted to see his owners again.

Lydia paid the bill with her credit card, while Harper walked the dog out to the truck, putting him in the second seat where he had laid out a clean fleece. Lydia joined him, and they headed home.

Once they drove up the driveway to the house, the gate code still working as it had before, they found the Sprinter van there. The two men waited outside, Danny smoking a cigarette which he quickly put out.

"Hey, guys, nice to see you. Let's go inside and talk. I've got Amos down at Sally's, I think. Have you checked in with him yet?" Harper asked.

Greg answered him first. "Yes, he's there. I told him what she was like. I'm sure he's gonna have fun."

Lydia inserted herself next. "She'll probably stay up with him all night long, playing crossword puzzles. She hasn't had a man in her house overnight for decades, I don't think," Lydia said.

"I think he can handle it," said Danny.

Once inside, the two men retired to their respective separate bedrooms. Lydia told Harper to take Venum and go upstairs and take a long, hot shower.

She walked in to speak to both men one at a time. She was first at Danny's door. "Harper's pretty exhausted, and I need to make sure he sleeps in tomorrow."

"So did you find out about the meeting?" he asked.

"You mean Harper didn't tell you when he asked you to come up here?" Lydia asked.

"No. He just said things had come up. That's Harper."

She nodded "Well, apparently Lipori is responsible for these people who have been up here, and he thinks it's a plot to kidnap me. That's the new news anyway. We've got Venom, we've got Harper back, and I need to see to it that he gets a full night's rest so that he can fully function. There's gonna be some tough decisions made."

"No kidding. He going to get the Feds or local police involved?"

"I think they're going to try to handle it. But that

decision hasn't been made. I think the fewer people who know about this the better for all of us. But please be on your guard. Don't take anything for granted. Question everything. You hear something, go check it out. You guys work together. Hopefully, you can get some rest, but my job right now is to take care of Harper."

"Well then, ma'am, he's in good hands."

She went next to Greg's bedroom and basically informed him of the same.

"You take care then. You've got a big job tonight, Lydia. I'm sure Harper will bounce back in the morning. He does that. He goes for it one hundred percent, and then he bounces back. Always been that way."

"Thank you, Greg."

She walked up the stairs slowly, suddenly feeling about ten years older herself. The energy she'd had earlier today was not there any longer. She was going to spend the evening doing everything she could to make sure Harper knew how much he was loved and how much she needed him.

CHAPTER 9

H ARPER WAS STILL in the shower when Lydia stripped off her clothes and joined him. In the steamy confines of the four glass and tiled walls of their inner sanctum, they found each other. At first, her hunger for him far outpaced his for her. She washed his back, shampooed his hair, used the water wand to rinse him clean, and worked the bath oils into his skin while the warm water covered them both. He was nearly non-responsive.

It didn't deter her.

She knew he'd been crying.

Had he gone too far round the bend? Were they all asking too much of him?

"Harper, look at me, please," she whispered to his back.

He turned, peering down at her.

Her hands brushed over his scars, his tats, as if she could wash away all the worry and stress, all the pain and guilt he felt. She felt as though all the years of his service had come crashing down, and he was regretting everything he did. Second-guessing all his decisions of the past. He'd set the bar so high for himself he didn't allow for unusual circumstances to force a mission onto a different path, to accept the forward motion evil takes as it pulls the web closer toward them both. However, he'd get it in his sights, get it just close enough to quash the energy and negative lifeforce it held. He had a powerful connection to Dr. Death. She remembered they'd talked about it before.

Then she remembered something else. There was that day when he told her about his mother's suicide and how it made him feel. He was overseas when it happened. He couldn't save her. That was always what he feared most, not getting home in time, not being there. Letting people down.

It was not a memory she thought he'd appreciate, but the memories were coming back now. Maybe the stress and pressure was bringing them on. Whatever the cause, she'd be grateful for it, but she wouldn't force anything.

"Harper, I didn't forget everything. Little things keep coming back to me. You bring something out in me that was missing before. I remember the first kiss we had at the hospital. Do you?"

It was a complete pattern interrupt for him. He

nearly shook his head, thinking about it. Then he smiled, placing his palm against her cheek.

"How could I forget?"

"What I saw in you that day, when you were dealing with your dad, was a man of steel who still believed in love, in second chances. I saw a man who was tender with a father who probably made a lot of mistakes, a father who was dealing with his wife's death. He was losing his grip on life, but you didn't abandon him. You could have."

"Dad. That's been a trip to deal with him."

"I remember giving him a puzzle. He squealed like a ten-year-old, didn't he?"

"I'd forgotten."

"See, I'm not the only one with a terrible memory," she teased.

She turned off the water, which was starting to go lukewarm. "Let me dry you off. Come, sit."

She brought him out of the shower, sat him down on the padded chair at the vanity, and put oil on his scalp, running her fingers through and massaging his temples. She dabbed his body with the fluffy white towels she loved. She laced her fingers through his hair and kissed his ears, running her thumbs up his neck and squeezing his shoulder muscles gently. She kissed the base of his neck. "I used to do this, didn't I?"

He quickly turned and looked up at her in amazement.

"You *are* remembering, aren't you?"

"There was something about your face, something about your silver hair the moment I spotted you in Italy. It was familiar. I didn't know you, but I saw you as friend, not foe. And when you touched me, I wasn't afraid. It excited me, Harper, and it still does. Even without the complete memories. We've built that back. Our castle is coming back, brick by brick," she said as she kissed his neck again and smoothed over his chest with her palms, pressing her chest against his back.

"You're so tender. I never told you this, but when we first made love, in the beginning, I used to go to bed crying. I'd been so moved. I knew I was inexplicably caught, snagged. I was forever yours, Lydia. I would and still would die for you."

"Yes, I know this, my love."

She sat across his lap, straddling him. He held her waist in his powerful hands.

"So I'm going to ask you something. You said you would die for me, Harper. But what about this. Would you ever give up on us? Give up this life?"

"Never."

"Me neither. Hear my logic here. Let's not die for each other. I want you to live for me. I want to live for you. We signed on for better or for worse with each other. Sickness and in health, right?"

He waited.

"Nothing could ever make me stop loving you, Harper. I will never go away. I will always be here. There was something about cutting the flowers in Italy that was like going home, like I knew something else was out there. The more beauty I could take in gave me the reassurance that I was healing, that I would find that something else. And I did. You came for me. You knew even before you knew where I was. You followed your heart. Not your head."

"I was lucky. It was a lucky guess."

"Oh no. I believe that now. There wasn't anything that could separate us. No amount of evil. No tragedy too great. We made a choice, a promise to each other. That promise stuck with me, even though I didn't know that's what it was. You were always there, Harper. That's what I'm saying."

He pulled her mouth down to his and kissed her hungrily.

She whispered in his ear. "Come back to me, Harper. Let's do this together. We're a team. Nothing can stop us. We do this, and we fight this fight for all the innocent people who cannot. We open the doors and show them how good roots out evil. Whatever it takes."

"Whatever it takes."

"Are you with me?"

"Always, Lydia. Always."

She held his head in her palms again. "So let's not die for each other. Let's live for each other. Let's grab all we can get of this life and not let go. Let's fix what we can, and let others do the rest. Whatever happens, I want to do this with you. I married you for life. You're mine. And we'll be together even after that. I see that now."

He kissed her again, picked her up, and brought her into the bedroom. Both of them were still wet. Venom was slightly offended that Harper adjusted him off the bed with one giant sweep of his forearm. He groaned his objection to having to move just as Harper planted a huge kiss on her lips and laid her there.

They both chuckled.

"We'll have to get him a girlfriend so he learns what it's like," Harper whispered.

"He knows, I think. He knows you very well…"

He kissed down her neck and between her breasts. "What did I ever do to deserve you, Sweetheart?"

"You didn't marry someone else. You saved yourself for me, Harper. If you'd chosen another path, I wouldn't have kissed you in the hospital. You would have belonged to someone else."

"Man was I lucky."

"I think it's all skill. Two sides of the same man. Maybe I'm the same. But one side is stronger. Your capacity to love under difficult circumstances is far the greater skill. It doesn't take anything to kill, but it takes everything you've got to love like we do, Harper. Everything. We can't hold back. We go forward, no matter what. I don't love part of you. I love all of you. The good, the bad, and the neither good nor bad."

He chuckled with that.

"Thanks for not ruining the name of my favorite movie," he whispered. "So tell me, sweet Lydia, what is it you want me to do? Dare I ask you to say the words?"

"Hmmm. Let me think. Okay, I've got it."

"Tell me. I'm dying to know."

"First, you have to lie down on the bed. Fully stretched out, okay?"

He angled his head in puzzlement. "That's not what I was expecting."

"Just do it. Remember, you're mine to do with as I please? You have to do it."

He did so. She placed his arms above his head and made sure the pillow under his head was soft. "Do you want another pillow?"

"Only if I need to watch. You want me to sit up?"

"No, I want you to lie back. Remember? Like you told me?"

He furled his brow.

She straddled him as he placed his palms at her hips, feeling her skin. She felt the calluses of his trade. His erection was prominent between them, but they had not yet mated.

She placed his hands above his head again. "Leave them there. I dare you to do it. You aren't allowed to touch me, okay?"

"Is this sex or is this torture?"

"Oh, it's sex alright. Now, I don't want you to move a muscle. I'm going to do all the lovin', like you said to me, remember?"

"I do. You couldn't keep your hands still."

"I'm counting on you to do it, though."

She used her hand to grip his member and place him at her opening. His hardness lurched under the touch of her fingers. She braced herself, pushing against his hip bones and rising up on top of him, and then pressed down on him, taking him into her completely to his hilt. The delicious ripple of pleasure made her tingle all over. She sat up again and then came down slowly on him, while she looked into his eyes. She willed him to know her innermost thoughts, how wonderful he was making her feel, what being in her life was doing to her.

She leaned forward, kissing him deeply. He started to reach around to her backside, and she chastised him and pushed him back. She kissed him again, with his hands idly limp above his head.

Lydia improved the pace of their movement, riding him, tucking her feet beneath him, arching high and coming back down, moving from side to side so he could feel her insides.

He was getting fuller. Her internal muscles were starting to quiver. She was at the edge of ecstasy when at last he couldn't take it any longer, reached up, flipped her on her tummy, propped her hips up, and rammed himself into her from behind.

He was crazed with desire, pumping deep and quick. Her control was waning as she surrendered to the pleasure he brought her. He drilled into her with everything he had. In one final push, he spilled, biting her neck as he did so which gave her a tiny bit of pain, but all the pleasure.

"God, I love you, Lydia. Thank you for bringing me back," he whispered to her ear. "Don't ever let me forget this again."

"I won't. We love in the here and now. We love in the living, love for each other. There is nothing after that, Sweetheart. I'm here forever."

"Forever," he said and collapsed.

CHAPTER 10

G REG WAS THE first one to noticed Harper's twinkle toes, the fact that he looked perhaps twenty years younger than he had last night when he marched up the stairs. Harper had gotten up before anyone else and was making blackberry pancakes. He'd even taken Venom out for his morning pee and picked berries for them.

He was singing showtunes and slamming plates around the kitchen. Everyone in the house was awake, and it was only seven.

Lydia slipped by Harper, who wouldn't let her pass without a feel down her nighty through her robe, and after extracting his payment, he went back to the pancakes. She made coffee and then watched him work.

"Well, what in the name of Dobermans has gotten into you? Did you deposit that old self outside or something last night?" Greg asked.

"That's about right. We got living, breathing people here. Time to feed everybody. We want to be stuffed with coffee and a sugar high so we can think. We're going to strategize and plan, Gents. We have a mission to accomplish."

Danny peeked around the corner, wearing his red, white, and blue pajama bottoms. His hair had morphed into a ducktail planted in the middle of his head.

"I can't believe this. You're crazy, Harper. You cook?"

"Oh yes, I cook. Don't I, Mama?" he said slapping Lydia on the butt.

She felt her cheeks flush. "Yes. He cooks. Behold!"

Harper made eggs and bacon, and Lydia brewed another pot of coffee since the first one was consumed before they sat down.

"In my house, growing up," Harper started, "we used to hold hands and give thanks. My parents weren't good role models for much, but this one tradition, I suddenly appreciate more than others. So indulge me," he said as he took Lydia's hand on his right and grabbed Greg's on the left. Forming a circle, the boys scanned each other's faces. Lydia could see a question forming there.

"I want each one of you to say something good that happened in the last twenty-four hours. Just one thing and then we go to the next person. I'll go first. I am thankful for the loving arms of my lovely wife, Lydia, and her conniving ways. I know I said one, but I have another. I'm thankful for Venom's strong constitution, for his unfailing loyalty. Good to have you back home, Venom."

The dog cocked his head but stayed sitting to attention next to Harper's chair, hoping for a table scrap.

"Greg?"

"Wow, this is so unexpected. Never done this before. I'm thankful for being able to stay in the legend's home. Now I can tell all my friends who served with him that he is master of his castle and has built himself a home fit for a king. Harper, if I win the lottery, tell me you'll sell this home to me?"

Everyone laughed.

"The answer is no."

They laughed again.

All eyes were on Danny.

"I'm thankful for sincere friends, for people we can count on, for people with values I aspire to. I appreciate the leadership, Harper, and the inspiration, Lydia."

"Something go on while I was in D.C.?" Harper asked her.

"Oh, lots went on. Not sure how inspiring I was. I was a mess. A total mess. These guys helped me get out of my meltdown. And for that, I'm grateful. I think when what you truly love is threatened, it makes you appreciate them more. I appreciate and love all of you, some more than others," she said as she winked at Harper.

"Fair enough. Now let's dig in before it gets cold."

The huge breakfast so early in the morning made Lydia feel like she should go back to bed, but she and the Team Guys cleaned up the kitchen while Harper made some calls to D.C.. She tried not to listen but thought she heard a promise that he'd take her back in a couple of days. She wasn't looking forward to that.

The kitchen was clean. Danny took Venom out into the garden on the leash. Back inside, more coffee was brewed, and they took places in the living room.

"I've talked to the admiral this morning. He's getting permission to conduct a Silver Team mission since our current circumstance is directly related to the last mission we went on. So here's the deal. I need to take Lydia back to D.C. to have a conversation with Lipori. They want him on tape admitting to the things he told me. He's demanding an audience with her, so they think, and I agree, it will look like we're trying to comply with him and that he's in control."

"But you're in control, right?" said Greg.

"Sort of." Harper took another gulp of his coffee. "He's willing to give up the couple who have been hounding our property here. Told us they were paid to get Lydia, bring her back for a price, to Africa, to

Benin, in particular. We have no intention of letting that happen, and Lipori knows that. We've told him no deal, but he's insisting he talk to Lydia himself."

"What's he expecting, then? What do you have to deal with?"

"I don't think he cares much whether the couple lives or dies. He's already turned on several of his friends. He wants out of prison. He thinks maybe we'll give him that."

"Holy cow, Harper. We can't do that!" Lydia blurted out. "You know he'll just jump back into something else."

"We do. In fact, we're counting on it. But we have to set it up so it works in our favor. I don't doubt he has other teams, ready to do things either here or in Europe. Maybe you can get that out of him, Lydia. But don't believe anything he tells you. He's a narcissist, only really cares about himself."

"You're going to go in there with her, right?" asked Danny.

"If he'll let me. Something tells me, though, he won't. We'll have it on tape."

"So how does this work, then?"

"He has the interview with Lydia, and then he gives up the couple. If they can work out a deal, he'll reveal more. What he's doing is trying to obtain his freedom. We want to encourage him that it might happen, if we get enough of a prize worth letting him out."

"Harper, aren't you playing with fire, though?" Greg asked. "He's outsmarted everyone up until now. He had to have had this couple lined up before he got arrested, his fail-safe option."

"Could be. Could be he has many. We're not sure how he's getting messages out. He's not allowed to have a cell, have access to the internet. Somehow, he is."

"Hate to say it, but I'd suspect one of those max prison guards. Money talks, you know," added Greg.

"We'll find the source. He may even give that person or persons up himself. But this is the course of action the president and the admiral want us to take. Our mission is to capture all his accomplices—or nearly all of them, at least the ones who are threatening us here—and then catch Lipori doing something he shouldn't, giving us the option to put him away for good."

"You mean, as in prison, not—"

"Exactly," Harper said too quickly. Lydia noticed the ruse. He was actually considering doing something more lethal. That worried her.

"So where do we come in?" asked Danny.

"I want you on the Silver Team. I've been okayed to invite you. They're sending me the contracts. You'll be pleased with the details."

Danny looked pleased. Greg held his approval back a bit.

"You guys are to remain here, along with two others I'm bringing up from Coronado. You don't know them, but they've been on three ops with the Silver Team already. You'll be using this home as your headquarters. You'll guard the place, and when we're ready, you'll engage the couple and take them out. No law enforcement. My understanding is the FBI will be told, but unofficially."

"Harper, are these Americans we're talking about?" Greg asked.

"Not sure."

"Doesn't that complicate things if they aren't American citizens?"

"Technically, it complicates their stay here if they're not. Do you suppose we could enforce the law by chance?"

Lydia agreed it was a valid point.

"I have a question. I don't have to pretend to be kidnapped, do I? That wasn't part of the plan, was it?"

"Hell no."

"Then she's the bait," said Danny.

"Not really. Only when he's in a secure location will she talk to him. She's not going to have to deal with him outside of that cell."

"You think he'll keep his promise?" Lydia asked.

"He'll bargain. He's going to try to surprise us. That's why I need everyone on their toes. We need to be one step ahead of them, all the time."

"If he gets out, he won't be set free in the U.S., will he?" Lydia asked.

"We're working out a deal where he'll be turned over to the Italians."

Lydia had a sinking feeling about this plan all of a sudden. "This is your idea, your plan, or was it—"

"It's mine. I think it will work. I'm counting on the fact that he'll do anything he can to gain his freedom. That's the prize he wants."

Greg and Danny were tasked with looking over the property for other poison drops. They found a handful, but all in the front yard area. Nothing was found in the rear yard where the vegetables and flowers were. That area was fully fenced to make it deer proof, so it was thought Venom might be able to run loose there, but never in the front yard.

Lydia and Harper took the dog down to the hospital for his blood test. His toxicity levels were improving dramatically.

Harper made arrangements for their flights to D.C. in two days. Sally was brought into the conversation. They brought up Carl Womack and a new team member, Mallory Cruz, who had tried out for the SEAL Teams and gotten through BUD/S but was placed on hold until they could find a place for her. Rather than wait, she opted to join Silver Team, even though she was the youngest of the crew. Her specialty was that she posted the highest scores in sniper school, beating out all the older competition hands down. Harper wanted that expertise on his side.

Hamish and others might come later, but with this crew, they could prepare while Harper and Lydia were in D.C..

The appointment was scheduled. Lipori promised to give out the location and name of the couple working in Sonoma County and assured them there were no others. But he wanted that interview with Lydia first.

Just as Harper had told her, it all hinged on her.

CHAPTER 11

THE HARDEST PART of leaving their home in Sonoma County was saying goodbye to Venom. He'd only been home for two days since his recovery at the hospital, and although they both tried to give him the lion's share of attention, whenever he wanted it, it was still difficult, perhaps even more so for Harper than Lydia.

The black sedan took them to Santa Rosa airport where a special chartered jet waited for them for the trip to Washington, D.C.. Once they settled in and the plane began its takeoff, Lydia's nerves encroached on her peace of mind. Her stomach began to churn.

They held hands as the forward thrust sent them into the air. There would be one stop over to refuel and then the remainder of the trip without a stop.

They were offered light refreshments, but Lydia couldn't keep anything down. She'd had an annoying feeling in her stomach for days now, ever since Harper left to go back to D.C..

"I felt bad about not spending more time with him. I wish we could've brought him," she said to Harper.

He was having a whiskey, a little early in the morning for that, but these days, Lydia didn't criticize anything, and she assumed Harper was doing the same.

"Me too. But he's better off and safer at home. The boys will spoil him crazy. I know they're on the lookout for anything suspicious, so in a way, this whole trip would be a lot easier if this couple would just show up while we're gone and get the piss knocked out of them."

She chuckled. "Or they'll stumble on Sally's house thinking it'll be an easier ride, and she'll knock the piss out of them."

They both laughed at that.

"I'm glad you've lightened up about all this," he said.

"Well, it's partly because I don't know what I'm getting into. I've learned around you sometimes not to ask too many questions. Just go with the flow. I can't say that's my preference. So let me ask you this. Are you able to elaborate anything or give me some pointers?"

He didn't look her in the eyes when she asked this. She knew he was hiding something. Not anything that would cause her harm, perhaps something that would protect her.

"Not sure I can tell you what to do. He's very smart, he reads people well, and don't forget, he's lived around you for more than two years."

"That's the only part I remember."

"Lucky that you did. You helped round up a lot of would-be terrorists. It helped the case against Lipori, him being associated with so many involved in these splinter groups, coming from all over Europe and North Africa."

"Just doing my job. They also wanted to make sure I wasn't part of it. Cooking and keeping house wasn't aiding the cause."

"Different for you. You were married to me, and you are an American. They've convicted housekeepers, lovers, and landlords who knowingly rent to these groups."

He hesitated and then asked something Lydia could tell he'd been thinking about for a time.

"I need to ask you a question though. It came up during the briefing. Were the two of you intimate?"

Staring into his warm eyes, it was difficult to discern what was on his mind. Surely he didn't think she'd slept with Lipori!

"Of course not. We were friends. He was like my benefactor, more like a brother, although he's about my age but very rich. I was still shaken up, not knowing who I was or where I was, and I just had no recollection of where I'd come from. He offered to take care of me while I convalesced. I mean, flower gardening outside of Florence, selling them at the market, cooking, reading, and relaxing, what's not to like about that? I had no idea I had this other life. Well, let me correct that. I knew there was something else. I knew there were special people in my life. Just couldn't recall where and who."

"So did he question you a lot?"

"Yes, but every time I got to feeling uncomfortable, I told him, and he stopped. I mean, Harper, I can't really say I have any complaints."

"Don't take this the wrong way, Lydia. Groomers are good at taking good care of their prey. I know you want to think he treated you well because you're a decent person and you deserved it, but he's a cold-blooded killer, and in his heart of hearts, he only cares about one person, and that's himself. If I could caution you about anything, I would caution you about that. He may appear to be reasonable, even kind, maybe even say he has an attachment toward you. I'm expecting that. But don't fall for it."

"Just how should I be? Should I react harshly? Now that I know what he did and that he took me away from the life that I loved, the people I loved?"

"I would maintain your honesty and your integrity,

only lie to him if you must. Always protect everybody else in the group, yourself included in that. He'll be able to tell when you're lying. These 'artists' do that very well. More skilled than their interrogators, usually. It gives them energy, excites them to deceive people. Don't tell him anything that will make you unsafe. You don't want to give him any information he doesn't already have. But he's gonna throw some things at you that are going to surprise you."

"Like what?"

He squeezed her hand and brought it up to his mouth, giving her palm a kiss.

"Sweetheart, if I knew that, we wouldn't be on this plane. We'd be doing something else." He wiggled his eyebrows for special effect.

She got it loud and clear.

"Okay, so be honest, be open, listen skeptically, but be compassionate? Do you think that would disarm him? I mean, it seems like a natural way for me to be."

"I'd agree with that. Just make sure the compassion doesn't translate to him that you care for him and try not to show that you care for me, even though he's going to know that you do. You don't want to arm him with some information he could use to hurt you later. To draw you in, to compromise you. To start telling tales and drive a wedge. He's gonna want to do that. He's gonna want to drive a wedge between you and me.

He thinks you're the softer one of the two of us. And I don't think he's right, do you?"

She giggled. "I think people underestimate me all the time. I think it's sort of what I've lived with my whole life. Many women feel the same. It's a secret weapon maybe. I notice things, I observe things about people, and I intuit certain things, keeping everything to myself usually. But somebody like him, who can turn off and on, who can cold-bloodedly kill women and children. Children! I saw the pictures. They showed me all the pictures."

She shivered at the remembrance of that day of questioning. The most horrible day of her life—that she could remember.

"Did you recognize anybody who was killed?"

"It's been a while, but no, I don't think so. I really didn't want to look. So trust me, I didn't study the scene. But I did see the pictures of those little children that I must've helped, given them baby checks and inoculations, advising their mothers. It was mostly women and children, very few men. They were sitting ducks, Harper. There was no reason for this loss of life. Did they ever figure out why this warlord wanted to do this?"

"I think General Okubo had informants that told him these women and children were perhaps families of warriors who were in opposition to him. I'm not sure he kills just for the sake of killing, but I think revenge killing is rampant throughout most parts of Africa where there is armed malicious and military conflict. It's warfare on steroids, except they're getting anti-tank missiles and javelins and all kinds of arms from larger nations who want to see them get themselves blown up or destroyed. People make money on the murder and slaughter of women and children. It's despicable. And those who try to help are left in the middle. After a while, on the Teams, I was proud of the work we did as far as rescuing people, getting the bad guys out, and bringing them to their ultimate end or interrogation rooms for the government. However, there was always ten more people standing behind them ready to take their spot. It was a never-ending cycle. I wonder if we did any good at all."

"But of course, Harper, like in all things, you weren't giving all the details. Just enough to do your job. Thank goodness all those men who died in World War II weren't told all of the things their superiors knew before they went into battle. It's a necessary evil. Doesn't make it very palatable, and I feel so sorry for them. But they signed up for it, didn't they?"

"Heroes always do, Lydia. That's what makes them heroes. They do what they're called to do. We need protectors like that. Otherwise, we have complete lawlessness, anarchy. They do it no matter what the danger is. That's why their sacrifice is so utterly fantastic. You and I would do well to never forget their sacrifice. I know I can still see the faces of every man I served with who didn't come back or who came back a little bit twisted. That's not hard to do."

She leaned against his shoulder, and he put his arm around hers.

"I'm just so glad you're back. I'm going to try to catch a little nap if you don't mind, and then I'd like to get something to eat when we land."

"You got it. I'll wake you up when we do."

Lydia's dreams were filled with fire and bloodied screaming. It was something she remembered when waking up in the hospital. Every time she closed her eyes, that's what she heard and felt. Every person who'd walked into the room scared her, even though the nurses were all very gentle. She had been taken to an exclusive hospital run by Catholic nuns. Every person still initially looked like an enemy to her at first.

Later, it was explained to her by several of the nurses that she'd been involved in a terrible automobile accident. They told her she was an American living in a villa somewhere unknown, which happens, and had been involved in that horrible crash. Her loss of blood and the head trauma she suffered caused her to lose her memory, they said. They assured her this memory would return.

When she discovered the large scar on her chest, she was told they'd tried to save her heart, but in the end, they had to look for a transplant candidate and got one just in time, thanks to her mysterious benefactor. It was explained that some piece of metal had crushed her in the front seat, had one straight through her heart and lungs. Her lungs were able to skirt some of the damage, but the heart took nearly a direct hit, and although she had started to improve, it was going to fail eventually. The lack of blood would kill her. Her function was less than thirty percent, they told her.

In her dream today, she saw the grassy plains of Africa, or what she assumed was Africa. She smelled something, fire and blood. In her dream, she tried to look behind her. Someone picked her up and pulled her into a truck. That's when she blacked out and didn't wake up until she was clean, safe, and lying in a comfortable hospital bed attended to by nuns and nurses.

She remembered asking who she was and if she had any identification. She asked the nurses if anyone had reported a family member missing in the area, if anyone had inquired about a car accident. Nobody knew anything at all, told her all the contents in the auto were destroyed. Did this happen in Africa? She thought it was odd she would be driving through Africa, and they corrected her.

"No, no, Sweetie," they said in their beautiful lilting Italian accent. "You were in Florence, outside of Florence. That is where your accident was. Not Africa. We wouldn't take care of you here, you would be at a hospital there."

There were still so many questions. Maybe Lipori had some answers, not that she could trust him.

She drifted into a deeper sleep, and this time she had real flashbacks—burning huts, the smell of decay in the hot sun, and again, being pulled into the back of a flatbed truck. She could see thatched huts in the background and palm trees riddled with machine gun fire, their fronds hanging on strings of green thread. It was very different than Italy. Italy was arid and rocky. Africa was lush and green with red-brown soil and the smell of death all around.

She remembered the first time she saw Lipori after the accident. She'd been sleeping, and he was just there when she woke up. He'd brought flowers, had laid them on her chest. She wondered first if he was her husband or boyfriend or a lover.

"Who are you?"

"Georgie, you don't remember me? I am Jakob Lipori. We are friends. We are good friends. I was able to rescue you from the accident. I was following you from behind, and a very large truck veered off the road, sending you down an embankment. You hit a large olive tree. It was horrible. I pulled you out just in time before the car exploded. Do you remember any of this?" he asked.

She shook her head, and then she looked at the flowers.

"Yes, these are for you, Georgie. I don't know if you remember, but my parents are very wealthy. We were able to afford you the very best care. I don't want you to be afraid. All the bills are taken care of. But you must rest and get better. We have great adventures ahead of us!" he said with a wide, winning smile.

She was fairly certain, although her mind was still foggy, that she didn't smile back. It was just all too sunny and bright. And it didn't explain the carnage and death she had in her dreams. She knew there was something more, something much more evil out there. Just as she knew there was something or someone out there who would save her.

CHAPTER 12

"**Y**OU'LL DO FINE, Sweetheart. Just remember what I told you. Stick to the truth; don't reveal anything. He's going to tell you some things you don't want to hear, and I think just about all of them are going to be untrue. So don't fret about what he says. Suspend your disbelief. Do not trust him for one second."

Lydia knew he was telling her the truth. She also knew Jakob Lipori could be very convincing. He had an easy manner about him, and Lydia had fallen into his routine before when she didn't know any better. He probably counted on her still trusting him.

There was no way that she still did. But he'd test her.

The attendant walked her down the gray, brightly lit hallway into an anteroom filled with tables, looking like a cafeteria or a family reunification center. Everything was starkly white or dark gray, very clean, and with plenty of light. Even in the great room, there were skylights, which did much to make someone forget they were in a maximum-security prison. She was impressed.

Then the attendant led her down along a narrow hallway that was also well lit, but with fluorescent lights that buzzed. They passed a series of rooms covered in doors with a small window in wire glass. At one of the doors toward the end, she stopped, unlocked it, and let Lydia inside. There was a gray table in the middle of the room on one side. Hooks were embedded in it, presumably to connect the chains of a prisoner and keep them fully shackled. On the other side, where the attendant showed her a metal chair to sit in, there was nothing.

She had given her purse and all her belongings to Harper before she entered, but the attendant dutifully did a soft body search, not very intrusive.

"Okay, ma'am, you can sit here. We will bring him in just a couple of minutes. Do you have any questions?"

"Will somebody be at the door the whole time?"

"Yes, ma'am. Both doors. They'll be right outside. If you need anything, bang on the desk or raise your voice a bit, but they will be visually checking through the window. The prisoner will be fully shackled, both ankles and wrists. His wrists will be attached to the table here. He will be unable to reach across and touch you. You are also not allowed to touch him. And I know you've already been searched, but in case you're thinking about passing him a note of some kind, a weapon, or file, you'll wind up in jail if you try to do that. Not saying that you would."

For a prison guard, she thought he was rather friendly and non-threatening. She appreciated this. Her nerves were caving by the second. She needed all the courage she could muster, having never been in this position before.

"Okay, I think that's it. I'll just have a seat and wait. How long will the interview be allowed for?" she asked, looking up to him.

"I think you can take as long as you like. The rules here are a little soft on that respect, but if it gets to be over an hour, we may call it. You may have to reschedule. We generally don't have interviews that last longer than half an hour to forty minutes. Anything else?"

"What if I wanted to go back and have my husband come in and do an interview with him, again? He's seen him before."

"Well, he'd have to ask to make an appointment, and it won't be today. If the prisoner agrees, it could be tomorrow or the next day. But not today. We schedule these in advance, and we make staffing decisions based on the requirements we have for the day. I hope you understand."

"No, that's fine. I don't think it will be necessary."

She sat in the bright sterile room, feeling like a small child waiting in the doctor's office or the school nurse's office when she was in grade school. She was grateful it was clean and not grungy like a dungeon. She'd seen some of those in museums on display when she traveled. But this one, as prisons went, seemed to be well run. She guessed it was managed by an outside company, not by the Federal system itself. In a very unsafe environment, she felt relatively at ease.

Keys on the other side of the door across the room began to rattle, and soon it creaked open. Jakob Lipori, in a light blue and white striped prison uniform, walked toward her, his head bowed. His hair had gotten longer, hanging around his neck and shoulders. She had been used to seeing him with his distinctive ponytail. He appeared to have lost weight.

He wore slip-on plastic sandals and socks, and his feet were linked together around the ankles, no more than eight to ten inches wide so he had to shuffle. His wrists were clasped together by handcuffs and chains. One chain went from his wrist to around his waist and hung like a leash behind him so that, as he sat at the table, his guard secured it around the chair and locked it in place. The guard pulled Lipori's wrists forward in between the two metal braces and locked Lipori in place.

The guard briefly looked at Lydia and then back to Mr. Lipori.

"There is to be no physical touching. If at any time either of you wants to end this interview, all you need to do is call out to the guard or bang your fist on the table. There is a guard on her side of the wall and a guard on your side, Mr. Lipori. If anything goes on that's outside the rules, this interview will be terminated and future access might be restricted. Do either of you have any other questions?"

Lydia shook her head. Lipori raised his, gave a sexy glance Lydia's way, and shook his head no.

The door was locked behind the guard and the two of them were left alone.

Lydia's heart pounded, so much so she wondered if he could feel her pulse when her hands sat on the table, across from his.

Jakob Lipori made no secret of the fact that he found Lydia attractive. He scanned her upper torso, highlighting certain parts she would've found rude and insulting if she was in the general public or if they were strangers. It made her feel like a piece of meat. But of course, she was braced for the fact that Lipori was going to try to do something that would set her off-kilter.

"Well, Georgie, we made it at last. I was wondering

when you'd come back and see me." He smiled very cautiously. "Did you miss me at all?"

He was different, she noted. He was bitter, showing outwardly his evil intent. She'd always known him as half-gentleman, flirtatious, but not hard. This man sitting in front of her was not stable. It scared her.

"It's Lydia. I'm Lydia Cunningham. Georgie no longer exists."

"I see. Well then, in all due deference to you and your hulking husband, I will still call you Georgie, if you don't mind, in honor of the young nurse killed in that African massacre. She was your friend. Her name was Georgie. I liked her too."

Lydia wasn't sure what he was talking about. Lipori was wild in the eyes, his mind wandering, acting like a caged animal. She suspected he might be in near panic at being caught and incarcerated.

"As you know, I don't remember that village or Georgie, God rest her soul. But let's get down to business."

"Yesss! Let'sss," he said excitedly, lengthening his "s" sounds to sound like a snake. He began leaning forward, all too close.

"You asked for the interview. I'm here. I understand you're trying to work with your handlers to come up with some solution. They have given me some idea what you've proposed, but it was your wish that you make that request to me. So I'm here. I'm just here to listen. Understand, I don't have any decision-making capabilities or power."

"But you do. I'm sure you have requests. You want your husband to be safe, you want your dog to live, right? You want to have a hand in their safety. That's what I'm offering, with your permission."

Lydia backed up in the chair, crossed her legs, and stared at the wired window behind him. The guard was peeking through the glass, having to bow to get a glimpse of the both of them. He was tall.

"I'm not interested in chitchatting with you. I'm here merely to listen. We don't even have to talk very long. No need to take up too much of your precious time. I'm done being any part of your life."

Lipori leaned forward on his elbows, spread his hands, and showed her he was still securely tied. "I'm quite harmless here. And as for being part of my life or not, well, we share a history, Georgie. Perhaps the history isn't something you remember, but we have a history."

"Yes, I would say it's more like a tragedy, Mr. Lipori. More like a horror film."

He inhaled quickly, as if the sound of her voice was exciting to him. "I love horror films, especially the classics. I grew up in a dungeon, don't you know? My parents called it a castle, but it was more like a cell, similar to this one."

Lydia had some ideas what his childhood had been like and guessed it was no picnic. She reminded herself he would reveal things that were designed to throw her off and then change on her quickly to catch her off guard.

"Sounds idyllic." She tried not to make it snarky, but he growled and squinted at her.

"Don't make fun of Mummy and Daddy now. Poor things tried to manage me ever since I was little. Now they're rotting in prison. I'm so broken, Georgie. I can't speak of it." He placed his hand over his heart and furled out his lower lip.

He was completely crazy. She hadn't seen this side of him before. Apparently, incarceration was doing a number on his psyche, and this part of the puzzle falling into place gave her some ideas.

"So I gather your family wasn't close. Can we move on? I'm anxious to get to the purpose for this visit. Can we?"

"Call me Jakob." He smiled, so she nodded.

"You used to all the time, remember? Remember all the wine we drank together in Florence? Remember how many times I told you how beautiful looked in that blue bathing suit?"

She checked her memory and honestly didn't re-member those details, but she did remember a large pool out back at the villa, overlooking the flower garden she'd spent all day in. So she answered his comment with her own. "I don't remember any of that. I don't think we ever did that."

"Oh, that's right. You don't remember anything of Nigeria or Benin, do you? You don't remember the weekend we shared near the capital? At the five-star hotel? The Blue Heaven?" His eyes sparkled, and he licked his lips. "None of that you remember?"

In spite of herself, a frown creased her eyebrows. "Not a thing. As a matter of fact, I don't think it ever occurred."

"Would you believe it if I showed you pictures?"

"No. Pictures can be altered. Besides, you're not in any position to produce pictures."

"But I have friends. You know I have friends. You've seen some of them. In the grocery store, you remember those people? I know them very well. I also have other friends that are always waiting for their next orders."

"Was that a threat?" she asked him.

"No. Perhaps a promise. There's a lot at stake, Georgie. A lot on the line, wouldn't you say?"

"Okay, Mr. Lipori, I'm going to terminate this if you don't come forward and let me know what it is you want me to communicate. I'm not interested in cultivating a relationship with you, prolonging whatever fictional relationship you think we had in the past. This isn't Fantasyland, and as far as your requests, my understanding is you agreed to pull the couple off our house and our dog, our property, off of Harper and me, for me sitting down and talking to you. I'm here, so you let me know when this has sufficiently risen to the level of you permitting that awful couple to be prohibited from contacting me or my family any further. You let me know."

"Oh, you're so feisty. You know, when I first met you, you weren't. You were quite shaken. I was your knight in shining armor. You know I saved you, Georgie. Remember that?"

She looked at her hands folded on the table. Her urge was to stand up and leave the room, but she had a feeling he would allow her to do so, and then she'd kick herself all the way home for not taking advantage of the opportunity she had been given. "I'm getting tired of this. I'm not interested in what you think of me. I'm not interested in anything about you. I'm here just to serve a function. That is to transmit your communication to the people in the government that have a say to what your disposition is going to be. You help them, and perhaps they will help you. I'm not a party to this, except that you asked me to be here. So I've flown clear across the country just to sit here in front of you. Now, does that make you happy? Is that good enough for you?"

"It's entirely exciting. I didn't think you would look this good so soon. You are an attractive woman, Georgie. Haven't you ever thought about what we would be like traveling all over Europe, staying at all the finest places, drinking wine, having gourmet food? Jet-setting around the world, going to places most of the general public would never go to. You're an adventure seeker, a thrill seeker? Somehow I think you are."

There had been an element to this part of his personality when she lived in Florence, but his attentions hadn't been so fixed or pointed on her. It was now that he was coming on to her, and she was sure it was all lies. She was a means to an end for him. She was just his pathway out of this unbearable place.

"I've been patient enough. I don't want to listen to this any longer. Get to the point, Mr. Lipori. This is your last chance. If you don't think I'm gonna walk out of here, you're wrong."

She absolutely had had enough of him and his games and didn't want to do this anymore. He'd quickly crossed the boundaries she set for herself.

"What is your request? I will take it to the other side, and then we will get back to you."

"You will get back to me?"

"No, I won't. It will be somebody else. I don't plan on ever stepping inside this room again. So once again, let me know what it is you're asking for."

"I'm not sure you knew everything about our mission in Africa. So indulge me while I tell you a couple of things that might surprise you. We were quite close. We worked on the mission together. We liked each other. We even went to trainings in the capital city on several occasions, and we pushed for funding from the U.N. representatives who visited the mission. I mean, we worked well and generally liked each other. You trusted me with lots of valuable information about life, about your husband, about what he liked, what it was like to sleep with him—"

Lydia's radar began to buzz.

"Mr. Lipori, that's not appropriate."

"I began thinking about what it would be like to take a woman away from this big war hero who had rained Hell down on some of my little brothers and sisters in the Middle East. You would be my war prize."

"This is nonsense. I can see this was a waste of my time." She turned away, as if to stand.

"Well, I'm sorry, but it comes with the territory. I know you love your little family. You see, I don't think they've been honest with you. I don't think your husband's been honest with you. He knows what I'm about to tell you. I told him when he was here. Are you interested in hearing it?"

She already knew she wouldn't like anything he was

going to say next. It was all designed that way. She was being set up to be shocked. But, of course, her curiosity got the better of her. She knew afterwards there would be lots of regrets if she didn't, and she had worked on feeling the courage Harper had exhibited in his job. She wanted to show her fearlessness, so, perhaps at the expensive her own soul, she asked him to recount it.

"That's better. I like it when you allow me to say things. I grew very fond of you, Georgie. In fact, the more we worked together, the more I realized you were probably the only woman in the world for me. How could somebody like me, a terrorist, win the heart of a young nurse? Well, you told me about your husband and what a big wonderful man he was, a Navy SEAL no less, and how he made your world special. I heard the stories, and I knew I could do better. Because what I wasn't hearing in all this dedication and honor and duty was a passion for life. Not the passion for life I could give you."

He was completely deranged. There was no way she would have discussed intimate details with him or anyone, even a woman friend. He suffered from living in an alternate universe. He was a cretin. His mental illness had progressed significantly during his lockup. In spite of herself, Lydia interrupted him again.

"You're wrong. You're absolutely wrong. And I don't think we ever discussed this."

"Well, the die had already been cast, and the village was going to be raided. I knew what day it was going to happen, because I was going to join in the raid. We were going to make a statement. It was a statement to one of General Okubo's traitors, who had family in the village. It was the one way he could get even with the traitor, and the traitor would not be able to get him back."

Her stomach was lurching. She was finding it hard to breathe. "I'm not interested—"

"So I devised a plan so that you and I could escape. I could still participate in the raid, but you and I would escape, and I had men available to take us safely to our destination."

"What destination?"

"That's not important right now. But the bottom line is I planned to rescue you. And, in a way, I did."

She got angrier and angrier the longer he told the story. She wondered if Harper knew this. He had never told her. Thinking maybe he'd just lose energy, she allowed him to continue.

"Okubo showed up right on time. You and I had been doing something out in the garden as was planned. Then the slaughter began. You were so afraid. I told you I could get us out, but then he appeared, and before I could stop him, he shot you in the chest, demanding I join him. My men picked you up and cared for you until I could return. I thought the general had murdered you."

In a twist, Lydia realized that Harper had indeed killed the right man. She couldn't wait to tell him.

But the rest of his story was too much. She began to stand up.

"Georgie, if you value the life of your husband, you'll sit back down. We had a deal."

Lydia knew she'd regret her decision. She began to shake. "I don't believe it. None of this is true. You participated and helped plan the raid."

"True," he said matter-of-factly. "But I always planned on taking you with me, safely. You were quite shaken, and you clung to my arms like I was your only lifeline to this world, and I was, you see. You begged me to save you. You also begged me to save one of the pretty nurses. Maybe it was Georgie."

Lydia felt cold as ice. There was a tiny flicker of flame inside, in danger of igniting the whole room.

He was still trying to convince her. "I lifted you in my arms and ran across the campground, into the back of the truck, and off we went. There was a field hospital, very well equipped, used by several of the militia leaders, a secret place with a good doctor there."

But a voice tickled in her ear. Something she remembered Harper said.

"Don't react. No matter what he says. Don't give

him the pleasure of reacting. You're stronger than he is. Remember that, Lydia."

Just listen and get on with it. It was the hardest thing in the world she could do, but she heard him out. This time, though, she wouldn't look at his face. He tried everything in the world to get her attention, moving his head around and looking at her from the side and clicking his fingers, whistling. She refused.

"That's quite a story," she said to the table. "And what is your request?"

His reaction told her she'd surprised him.

"Did you hear me? I saved your life."

"I heard you. It's impossible for me to believe that. I just can't. Such a horrible story. Such a waste of human life. You're responsible for it. And for this, you think you should be rewarded with your freedom? Are you crazy? How did you think I'd react?"

"But the wound in your chest, you should not have survived. It went straight through the left side of your heart. It pierced your lungs. You would've been dead in thirty minutes if I hadn't taken you to that emergency facility. We got you patched up enough to transport you to the coast, like I had planned. You were unconscious, you were bleeding, you were turning chalky white, and your lips were turning blue. I thought mine would be the last face you would ever see. But you were strong. With my help, you made it. You're alive and well because of me."

He was nervous. She stared back at him with as much steel as she could muster.

He didn't deserve to live. She was being asked to reward him for being a despicable human being. She should be aiding in his demise, not the other way around. But she remembered she had to protect Harper, Sally, Venom, and the others. This crazed man, this demonic being would never stop unless they could get him into a trap and contain him once and for all. There was no real negotiating with him.

"Why should I do this for you? Beg for mercy for you?" she finally asked him to shut him up.

"Because I spared your life once. Now if you can help me, you can spare mine. I won't last long in this prison. They will kill me. They will find a way. I will give you the couple, whatever else you want, and I'll call off the dogs. But I want my freedom. You tell them that. I want to be turned over to the Italians, like what has been proposed."

"So why did I have to come all this way for you to tell me this?"

"I wanted to tell you, in person, that you owe me your life. For the love of the man you married, I am granting you that one wish, that you be able to spend the rest of your life with him. I give you that, if you give me my freedom."

She rose, not looking back at him, but she vowed that, if given the chance, she would end him. She was suddenly grateful she didn't have her memories back and hoped she never would.

CHAPTER 13

LYDIA LEFT THE interview room, feeling suddenly dizzy and sick to her stomach. She figured she'd stood up too quickly, yet vowed to be steady to the door and through the doorway into the hallway beyond. When she heard the clanging of the keys behind her, she relaxed. She wasn't going to give Lipori the satisfaction of knowing he'd upset her.

She still felt dizzy and shaken as she wandered down the hallway toward the lobby area. At one point, the guard grabbed her by the arm and held her steady. She'd been lilting toward the wall, brushing her fingers over the white and gray paint, trying to keep herself righted. Her stomach was still doing flip-flops.

"Are you okay, ma'am?" he asked her.

"I'm fine. I just—I just got up too quickly. I was sitting there for a long time. How long?"

"Nearly an hour, ma'am. Do you need to sit down?"

"No, I'd like to get back to the lobby. Get back to my husband."

The large open area was upon them, the bright lights suddenly unkind to her eyes. The demanding flashes seared into her brain, sending another wave of nausea through her. She hesitated, the guard helping her stay on her feet, but then began to feel sicker and asked for a restroom. He began walking her to the side of the room, where she saw the signs, but she couldn't make it. She doubled over and threw up all over the floor. Contents of her stomach spilled out over the floor.

"I'm so sorry."

"It's quite alright, ma'am. It happens. We see all kind of things in here. Are you sick, though? Did you touch the prisoner?"

"No. I did not." She stopped. A new course of worry, adding to all the other confusion, enveloped her. Could Lipori have poisoned her somehow? She ruled it out as folly. Her active mind playing tricks on her.

"Well, never you mind. I'm sure when we get you to your husband, you'll feel better."

"I just need to get home. I need to get away from this place."

"Yes, ma'am. I fully understand. Come on, just a little bit farther now. Let's get you to the lobby, to your husband. Don't worry about the mess. We'll get someone here to clean this up. Are you still able to walk?"

"Can you help me? I'm weak."

"Are you going to be sick again?"

"Maybe. I don't know." But she did feel better. Perhaps this was from the lunch they'd eaten on the flight.

"You need to go lie down, get your feet up. Here we are. I'll get you some water in just a minute. Here's your husband, ma'am."

She continued to walk, wondering where Harper was. She kept seeing Lipori's murderous eyes, hearing all the lies he was telling himself and her. She realized he never could be controlled. He was many times more dangerous than he had been before. The transformation was stark.

Putting one step in front of the other, she thought about their problem, their solution. No matter what they promised him, he would be incapable of sticking to anything set up. He was a wild semi-feral animal with no moral compass. He didn't care about anything or anybody but himself. He was deranged, evil. He belonged in a box forever. She had to tell Harper. She had to let him know.

Lipori wasn't like the Jakob she knew in Florence. Perhaps it was the interrogations and solitary confinement. He was obviously very sick. He was a man desperate for release. And he was even more dangerous than he had been before, because he wasn't rational. That meant they couldn't predict what he was going to do next.

Harper came running to her side as soon as he saw her. He shouted at the guard, "Did that goddamned sonofabitch hurt my girl?"

"No, sir. All they did was talk."

"I'm okay, Harper. I'm so glad to see you. I'm sorry I'm so weak—" She couldn't continue.

"It's okay, Honey. I'm here now." And then to the guard, "What happened?"

"I'm not sure, sir. He didn't touch her. They just talked, honest. She kept it tight until she walked through the door, and then she just collapsed into the wall."

"That fucker. Lydia, are you okay? Lydia, talk to me, Honey. What's going on? Are you okay?" Harper pulled out a Kleenex and wiped the edge of her mouth where some of her vomit had deposited.

"She's sick?" he asked.

"Yes. In the hall back there. She just let it go. Couldn't make it to the bathroom."

"Lydia, Sweetheart, let's sit down here please."

He took her to one of the plastic couches. It had holes stuck into with pencils, and someone had ripped a tear so, as she sat, she felt the sharp edge of the plastic on the back of her thigh. The room suddenly smelled of antiseptic and air freshener. The lights were too bright. She thought she might become sick again.

"Talk to me, Lydia, please. Should I take you to the hospital?"

"No. It's the lights or something I ate. It just came on me all of a sudden. I'm better now, but it was horrible, Harper. The man is horrible. He's a monster." She clutched at his chest, burying her head under his chin.

"What did he say?"

"He just told me about the awful village scene. I think that made me sick. He kept trying to convince me that he cared about me, that he saved my life, and I just don't buy any of it. I just can't. He's responsible for the slaughter of all those people. I just—" She sat up and looked into her husband's eyes. "I don't want to give him anything that he wants, Harper. He doesn't deserve it. He deserves to rot in prison."

"But we have to find the people he sent after us, and somehow, he's still doing it. If we turn him over to the Italian authorities, they'll take care of it."

"What if he gets out? What if he escapes? He's so dangerous, Harper. I fear we're looking at the next ten years of our lives trying to run from this fellow."

Harper put his arm around her, pulled her over toward him on the couch.

"It's okay, Baby. That's not gonna happen."

When she started feeling better and after she had a little bit of water, the two of them walked out into the parking lot and took a cab back to their hotel. Lydia took a shower, changed into her pajamas, and then went straight to bed, even though it was afternoon.

She woke up sometime later and heard the admiral's voice on the other side of the bedroom door. She opened the door a crack and waved at the two of them.

Harper was over in a flash. "Sweetheart, how are you feeling?"

"Much better, thanks. I'm so sorry about this."

"No worries. Do you need anything?"

"Maybe some water." She looked over at the admiral over Harper's shoulder. The man smiled back. "What are you guys doing?"

"We're planning, Sweetheart. Going over the interview, making strategy."

"I want to be a part of this. I'm supposed to be part of this."

"Absolutely. If you feel up to it. Can you slip on some clothes and come out and join us?"

She got dressed. The more she moved, the better she felt. She drank water Harper brought her, brushed her teeth, combed her hair, and examined herself in the mirror. She noted she was still pale, but pink was starting to return to her cheeks. She had underestimated his effect on her. She should have prepared herself better.

As she entered the living room, the admiral stood, giving her a concerned look.

"Admiral Patterson, this is my wife, Lydia. She's not feeling very well. The interview was quite hard on her," Harper said.

Patterson stood and gave her a bow but didn't approach. "I'm so sorry you had to go through that, my dear."

"Thank you," she said as Harper helped her sit down in their circle of three. He sat next to her, and Patterson took his seat across from them.

"We are just now discussing his disposition. You did well. We got a lot of things on tape. I think he did a pretty good job of incriminating himself for several lifetimes."

"But are you going to free him? I think he's too dangerous to let him lose. You can't."

His answer frustrated her. "I agree. But the quickest way to get you guys some relief is to locate and capture the couple who have been after you in California. He's useful to us if we can get their information out of him. And he's promised."

"You can't trust a thing he says. Don't do that."

"I do understand how you feel. He's pure evil, for sure. But we have ways of seeing to it he won't be able to get to you two. We're planning it now. You don't need to worry about that, Sweetheart. Your part is done. You did the heavy lifting. Now we're putting things in place to act on all that information you helped us get. Thank you, and I'm so sorry."

"He's got something planned. I know he does."

"He told you that? I didn't hear—"

"I can just tell."

"Lydia is very intuitive. You forget, they spent a couple of years near each other. She knows him," added Harper.

"Yes, I'm aware."

"But he's not the same man, Admiral. He's twisted. Bent. I don't think he's fully cognizant of what he's doing."

"Yes, and he's deathly afraid of staying in a jail cell for any extended period of time. You got that out of him. I think that's his motivation," Patterson answered.

"For now. Until he's free. Then he'll resort to what he was doing before. His word is not worth anything. I do not trust him."

"Then we'll make contingency plans," said Harper. "Lydia, we deal with these things a lot on our missions. We coordinate for Plan A, then have to go to Plan B, C, maybe even down to plan F when everything goes to hell. It's how we cope with so many variables. All we can do is discover all the many paths to safety there are and cover all of them."

He leaned over and kissed her forehead. She was grateful for his positive attitude, for his strength and warmth.

"I have to ask you guys something first," she asked. It was a question she needed to know. "Did you know he was going to claim we'd had a relationship? Almost as if he thought we were a couple? Did something happen I don't remember? Please tell me. Did something happen at the village I can't remember?"

Both men were silent. Her worst fears started marching loudly. Her stomach lurched again. She felt Harper tense up as the admiral glanced over to him for the answer.

"Honey, we don't know for sure. There is no evidence of that. We do believe he got you out of the village in time to spare you some of the things the other women had to endure. The honest truth is, we think he did save you from that. He'd spent a considerable amount of time organizing your exit and ultimate rescue. You getting shot, well, we weren't sure until your interview."

"So you knew he was going to claim this and you didn't tell me?"

Harper hung his head. "I made a mistake."

She pulled away from him and folded her arms on herself.

"Sweetheart, I had to weigh something very carefully. I showed you the tape, Lydia. I wanted to see if you remembered anything at all, and we're convinced you didn't. But what he thought, the ideas about him being able to take you from me, that you'd fall for him, I didn't play that part of the tape. I realize now it was a mistake. I figured you didn't need to know that. I knew that wasn't real. Remember, I told you he'd say things to throw you off? And he did. Just goes to show he doesn't really care about anybody but himself. He's a desperate, dangerous conman. I had to have you do the interview to get him to reveal his plan."

"If it makes any difference, Lydia, it was my recommendation," said Admiral Patterson. "I share some of the blame. He was against it."

Her heart began to soften, with one caveat. "Never again, Harper. You tell me everything, if I'm involved. Everything, understood? I don't want any surprises."

"Agreed. I made a terrible mistake. It was a judgment call, and I should have put you first. And you pulled it off, just like I hoped you would." He rubbed her back. "Once again, Sweetheart, I'm so sorry."

"You put the nail in his coffin," said Patterson.

She looked at the two of them. "I get it. But you need to know, I won't stop worrying until that man is dead. I have a problem making a deal with a killer, even if it costs me dearly. We can't live that way, Harper. Promise me you won't forget that."

He hugged her, and she heard his gentle sobs. "So sorry."

She pulled away. "Enough."

They explained that the Italian police were sending a detail from Florence, negotiated with the Italian Consul in D.C., who would be arriving within the week. Lipori would be transported to their custody.

"But let me ask you something, if you could, Lydia," asked Admiral Patterson. He drew several pictures out of a portfolio of telephoto shots of the compound, the villa in Imprunetta. "Do you remember this couple?"

Lydia looked over the photo and did recognize them.

"Yes, they came to the villa many times while I was there. They were friends of Lipori. I thought perhaps she was a relative of his. This is Maria and Garfur. Maria was Italian, and Garfur—I don't know, but he's Middle Eastern, perhaps Turkish? I never knew, but he had a different accent, while Maria's was definitely Italian."

"Did you speak with them, talk to them at length?"

"Not really. They were Lipori's friends. You remember, I didn't have any friends. I was mostly busy in the garden."

"Yes, but do you remember anything about what they were discussing when they were there? Any private conversations with them outside Lipori's ears?" Patterson asked.

"She followed me once out to the garden and asked me where I learned how to tend one, and I told her it was just natural, I guess. I asked her if she had one, and she kind of laughed, said no. Never been taught. I remember feeling she was envious of me, for some reason."

"Any other conversations?" he asked.

"Not that I can think of. No. They traveled a lot. They would come in for three or four days. Around olive harvest, a lot of the men came to help him do the pressing. They sold fresh olive oil, even internationally."

"Look carefully at the picture, Lydia," asked Harper. "Do they look familiar to you?"

She studied the two faces again then looked at several other photographs in the set. All of a sudden, it dawned on her. She had seen them before.

"Yes. They're the couple from the store. I never saw their faces. But I'm sure of it. Same build. It's them. Oh My God, that's them!"

"That was our guess. Lipori didn't mention them in the interview, either, did he?" Patterson asked.

"No, he did. He said they were good friends of his. Wow. Some way to treat a good friend."

"Just adds another piece to the puzzle. When the

Italian forces raided the villa, these two were not picked up. They escaped."

"You think it was arranged?" she asked.

"Probably not. Lipori did not want to get captured. I think they were just lucky," said Patterson. "It goes to show you, he uses everyone he can to leverage what he wants. Even his long-time friends. And you're right, Lydia, he cannot be trusted. But we're going to move forward carefully. Our main priority is to keep your home, you, and Harper safe, without putting you into some protection situation."

"Oh, I understand very well. I'm not happy about it, either. But I know we're bait. Sucks, but there isn't any other way you'll catch them."

After Patterson left, the two of them talked until Lydia grew tired again and retired. Her evening was filled with wild dreams, none of which she could remember in the morning. But she was satisfied there was a plan in place. Her warnings had been taken into account, and she believed in the successful plans Harper had executed over the year. She also knew it wasn't an exact science.

This was the price she was going to have to pay to remain in his life. He was always going to be putting his life on the line, putting the lives of his team on the line as well. Maybe she'd passed the test. Maybe she was part of the team now, just like he'd told her so many times lately.

If so, she was grateful for the opportunity to show how brave she could be. Because when it came down to it, she'd do anything to save Harper, just like he would do the same for her. It was part of their love story. It wasn't all roses and silver slippers. It was a bond between them, just like his Brotherhood of men. She was lucky to be a fully functioning part of that Brotherhood.

It was the stuff of heroes. She didn't realize until now that, in order to love a hero, she had to become one herself.

CHAPTER 14

T HEIR TRIP HOME was filled with messages and phone calls made from Harper's satellite phone. Lydia tried to lean back in the leather reclining seat and relax, but she was overhearing all of his plans, all of the items he had asked people to do while they were gone, setting up new routines and making the most of the fact that his team was now in full combat mode.

He finally set the phone down and rubbed his temples.

"Pretty exhausting, I'll bet."

"I'm used to it. A lot nicer with present company in this nice, comfy, and private space, high above the clouds. But still, I'm not a young buck anymore. It's also urgent, Lydia. I don't want to miss a thing."

She opened her eyes and stuck her feet in his lap. "I need a foot rub."

"My pleasure."

His fingers began kneading out all the pain in her

toes and causing more. She had to caution him to go a bit softer. It was wonderful the way his fingers worked over all her joints and tendons.

He watched her. "Do you have any questions about the plans?"

"No, I think I heard most of it. I think you've got it all spot on. But I had one question."

"Shoot."

"The one thing I don't get is why they haven't appeared since we've been gone. I mean, you would think they'd take this opportunity to mount an attack—at least on the home or Venom, something. They've just disappeared. Doesn't that seem odd to you?"

"Don't flatter yourself or think for a moment they're done. Maybe they're playing nice, maybe he told him to cool it for a while. I have no doubt once we return, if they're able to, they'll mount something."

"Do you think he'll warn them?"

"It doesn't matter. I will never trust him. We'll get them anyhow, if they show up. No worries, my love."

"I get the cameras and all the electronic devices. Did we figure out how they got the gate code changed?" she asked.

"Yes, they found a camera with a sensor installed in one of the trees overhanging. The monitor recorded the code that we punched in after we changed it. We located it two days ago and disabled it. And I had Paul

Taylor, he's our gadget guy, install a different device for the gate, both gates."

"Did anybody check the park next door?"

"They were all over that the next day, Sweetheart. We let the ranger know we'd been having some intruders on our property so they allowed us to stay there, two of the guys even camped out in a little storage shed they use for equipment, just to see if somebody would show up. We got cameras mounted on the shed. They will alert us if somebody trespasses. We also put a bead of sight down along the fence line, and if anybody tries to come over the top fifty feet, they'll be picked up."

"It's all monitored from the house?"

"Yes, ma'am. Set up, monitored, and tested. Apparently, it's like a whole control center there. You weren't planning on entertaining soon, were you?"

She smiled back at him. "No, I guess I'm going to be making pies and sandwiches for some hungry, hunky guys with tats and attitude."

"They better not, at least not around you. You let me know if anyone gets out of line."

"Oh, wow. You wouldn't be jealous, would you?"

"Just making sure they have the fear of God in them if they touch a hair on your body or make you feel uncomfortable. I'd be polite as could be their wives."

He continued to work, now closing in on her ankles. He chuckled.

"What? Are they swollen?"

"Nothing wrong with your ankles, honey, although I wish I could do this to you all over. No, I was just thinking that this part is kind of fun really. You know we have all these gadgets now. We get to test out all kinds of cool stuff on the Teams. And Silver Team is no different. Paul Taylor and a couple of the other guys are real gadget nuts. They can devise things you and I have never even thought about before. He and Coop have contests making listening devices out of household appliances or kids' toys. It's like a ritual whenever they get together."

"How's Sally taking all of this, or have they said?"

Harper laughed. "You know, I actually think she likes it. I think she would've been a great CIA agent or State Department special agent. She loves the action. She really does. She doesn't like to be pushed around. She's not a bully, but she loves standing up to bullies."

That seemed so like Sally. "She's missed her calling."

"Never too late to start. I think she's having the time of her life."

Lydia sat back, closing her eyes again and enjoying the massage.

"How do you like Patterson?" he asked.

"I can see why you trust him. He's pretty levelheaded. Would've been nice to meet the president," she said, leaning in his direction and stretching out her spine.

"Yeah, well, he's pretty busy right now, but you'll get a chance. Trust me."

"So you worked with him before when you were on the Teams?"

"Who? Collins? No, never met him until this year."

"No, Patterson."

"Before he made admiral, yes. He did ground support work for us, helping us stage two or three really high-level raids involving two separate Teams and Special Operators from Delta Force, others too. He doesn't much like the international force groups, but he's a good egg. A good man to have on your side. And he's levelheaded. He doesn't run off half-cocked. Very calm under pressure. I've never seen him get flustered. We need cool heads to work on this stuff."

"So this is all new then. They're trying to set up this new team and figure out how they're going to respond to things?"

"Well, it's been something the SEAL Teams have known about for a long time. There's always been talk amongst us in the Brotherhood that, if everything went to hell, we'd all jump in and do something. I mean, something other than try to, you know, run for a public office, which is an honorable way to attack some of the problems we have as a country and the leadership. But some of us, we can't do that. We're not ready to hang things up and quit fighting. That's all we've been able to do up until now."

"Now that you have Silver Team?"

"Yes, ma'am. An idea whose time has come, for sure. Gives us a chance, a fighting chance to combat some of these things. So now that we have to deal with all these threats coming in from all over, and it's like our country is a vortex, sucking all the bad guys in and making things so unsafe. They're coming from all over the world, just like Lipori said. You heard him on the tape I played you. He's right."

"They just walk right in."

"It's like taking candy from a baby. It's about time we start realizing we need to protect our own first. Before we go out there spilling our treasure elsewhere. Not that defending our allies and the innocents all over the world isn't still a good idea! What's different now is that we're actually making it a mission to keep the homeland safe other than just rules and regulations. Only good citizens follow rules. The bad actors don't give a darn. Rules were made for the good guys. We're here for the bad guys."

"I'm all for it. I think it's smart."

"I want to caution you about one thing, though, Lydia. It's still not official. I mean, we have the charter and everything, but the public doesn't know about this yet. Trust me, and in weeks to come, maybe months or a year or two, everybody's gonna know about us. But for right now, we aren't telling anybody except for those in the need to know. I think only people we absolutely know we can trust are in on this. And I'd like to keep it that way, for everybody's safety. It'll also make us more effective."

"Kinda like when the SEAL Teams were created in the 1960s, right?"

"Yup. They even named the first SEAL Team number 10 because they wanted the Russians to think there were nine other teams already formed. Wanted to make them think that they were behind the times. It was kind of an interesting strategy, don't you think?"

"I hadn't heard that. Makes sense though. So what do we do when we get back?"

"Well, I'm going to review everything they've done, and I asked them all to give me a list of items they have questions about or where they're blocked. I've got some funding coming, so we've got a cash account we can use. We've got extra personnel I'm allowed to hire, and even though we got a house that we want to live in, and as you said we're living in it like bait, we're not gonna make it look like we got a dozen people going and coming. That's going to be the trick."

"But the property is remote, Harper."

"Not from the sky. Not to the surrounding hills. We're wide out in the open and not close enough for help, either. So we have to make our own help, defenses. Sally's agreed to put some of us up, and there's a neighbor across the hill that has a perfect view of our property. There's also got several large structures, a water tower, and some tall trees that would be perfect for sniper perches."

"What do you tell these people?"

"We tell them we're DEA, looking to bust some druggies. Most people buy that."

Harper retrieved some waters and gave Lydia one.

"Speaking of snipers, I don't know if you're aware, but we brought on a female sniper, Mallory Cruz, and she's pretty damn good, the guys say. She beat out the entire class in her BUD/S unit, including the instructors. That's hard to do, unheard of."

"So she's going be a SEAL?"

He shook his head. "She's going be my girl. She's coming to Silver. I'm not going let those Bone Frogs get a hold of her and ruin her. She's on our team. You're gonna like her."

They were beginning to do their final approach to the airport when he got a call from Patterson. Lydia could heard the admiral's voice loud and clear.

"Admiral, I'm at your disposal, even though I'm still two thousand feet in the air."

"We got a tentative location for the couple. We did some digging. This didn't come from Lipori. Apparently, one of the neighbors in Florence came up with a name. I think this is our couple. They were granted a visa, so apparently, they're both Italian citizens. The visa was granted roughly thirty days ago. They'll be able to stay through the end of the year, but they gave a local address. We're gonna be having you check that out ASAP."

"Cool. Text me the address, and I'll send it on to Danny and Greg. Anything else?"

"For the transfer next week, we've got special guys replacing the local guards just to make sure there isn't any hanky-panky during the hand-off. When a guy has a few million dollars in the bank and doesn't hesitate to spend it, especially for his own benefit, it can make prison guards a little susceptible to some bribery. I'll let you know if anything comes of that. We also relocated him just in case he was working up to a crew at the supermax. He's located in a prison in Virginia, well outside of the city."

"Roger that. You have the handoff scheduled?"

"Done and ready. Vetted the Italians coming over."

"We don't need to have any direct communication with him, then? You're handling everything?"

"Not at this point, I don't think so. Oh, and you can tell Lydia, the president thinks she'd make a fine actress."

Lydia heard the squawking on the other end of the phone and shouted back, "Well, I'll take that as a compliment, Admiral, but I have no plans to go Hollywood."

She heard the admiral chuckle.

COMING HOME WAS the best part of Lydia's week. The boys walked Venom on his leash down to meet them at the upper gate. The dog was beside himself as he saw the black car and then was held back from dashing forward. Harper opened the rear door and allowed him to jump inside.

He commented to the driver. "I'm sorry, sir. The dog is just—I was afraid he'd jump up and scratch the car all to hell. Hope you don't mind."

"Understood sir, not a problem. He's one of you."

"Yes, he is," Harper said as he palmed Venom's ears and gave him a nuzzle. Venom sat across both of their laps, licking Lydia's chest, her arms, and her face, trying to nip her ear. He whined and then rolled over on his back and exposed his belly, so they both began scratching him.

"That a puppy, sir?" the driver asked.

"No, sir, he's eight years old, but he's always this way. He's the best dog in the world."

"Okay, well, you let me know if there's anything

else we can do for you," the driver said as he pulled to a stop, got out of the driver seat, and then picked up their suitcases from the trunk. Several guys came out of the front of the house and relocated the suitcases inside while Harper and Lydia extricated themselves.

Relief spread over her body. She stood there with her arms out, arching her back.

"This is the smell I've missed. Pure heaven. I missed this place so much, Harper. I don't think I'll ever travel again."

"You're lying, Sweetheart. I can always tell when you're lying. We'll be traveling. Just you wait and see."

CHAPTER 15

THREE DAYS AFTER Harper and Lydia returned home, Harper called an all-team meeting, including a big dinner spread at their house. The whole team was supposed to be there, except for two snipers, Carl Womack and Dodds Murphy. Womack would stay located up on the water tower over the next hill. Murphy was to remain atop the Park Service shed, camouflaged, watching his monitors for unwelcome visitors. This was considered light coverage, and Harper told them it would be the last time it would go that way. After all, they were about to begin a war, and control was the most important element.

Other than that, everyone was to show up. They provided a large turkey Harper was going to deep fry, a forty-pound prime rib, and lots of fresh vegetables. Lydia contributed five of her famous berry pies, with ice cream, of course. All the berries were from their backyard, as were the apples. Lydia was hoping they'd have enough leftovers to keep them fed for several days.

Sally came up the day before to help her with the baking. They'd done this before. She brought her own apron, and the two of them began cutting fruit and measuring the fixings for the pie mixtures.

"How's it going down there? You enjoying taking care of your three guys?" Lydia asked.

"Why? You think I don't enjoy having a man around? They're all real gentlemen."

"What do you talk about?" she wondered.

"All sorts of stuff. I know how to talk to a man when I want to. If he's respectful, Lydia. Shame on you! No, I like these guys. My kind of people."

"You have probably introduced them to your puzzles."

"Oh gosh, yes. When they're not working, but they work hard."

"I haven't seen what you've got down there, but does your living room look anything like mine?" Lydia asked as she pointed to her living room, which was literally covered floor to ceiling on two walls with monitors, consoles, scanners, wireless boosters, satellite receivers, and hundreds of miles of wires and cords, plus the shelving to hold it all. At all times, four people sat on the two sides, watching screens and listening to devices, running their computers, and analyzing sounds. It was the heartbeat and the pulse of the entire operation.

"No, it doesn't look anything like that. Well, maybe a little. My guys are pretty tight-lipped and don't talk about it. And that's okay. I just go out and do my work outside. I cook for them, and so far, they seem to be okay with my food."

"Are you kidding? They're in heaven, Sally!"

"And then at night, we play games. Puzzles sometimes. We don't watch much TV. They're really solid guys. They're actually no problem, other than the fact that I'm running out of hot water every day, mostly from the laundry I'm doing."

"I'm so grateful for what you're doing for us."

"Lydia, I know you'd do it for me if the roles were reversed. Besides, I'm right in there with you guys. I mean who's to say they wouldn't come after me just because I'm close to you or as a way to get to you. I'm a realist. I understand these guys are no-nonsense."

They paused. Then Sally asked, "Have you heard anything about Lipori?"

Lydia brought out two balls of dough she'd had chilled in the refrigerator and spread them out over the floured countertop for the both of them to roll and cut their piecrusts.

She shook her head. "Not a thing yet. The day after tomorrow is supposed to be the handoff. We'll see.

Everything's quiet. There's no chatter, except they did try to locate the couple, and the address turned out to be bogus. But they're still working on something. I just hate to ask Harper all the time, because he is right in the middle of so many things. I don't want to distract him."

The piecrusts were made and placed over the pie dishes, covered with plastic wrap to use for tomorrow. She was going to make two deep-dish apple pies, one berry pie, and a fresh peach pie. The pie plates were placed in the garage refrigerator. The fruit mixes they'd made were held in a sealed containers in the kitchen refrigerator until they could be put in the oven tomorrow.

Lydia's thought was to get all the work out of the way first, that way she could turn the kitchen over to Harper, who always wanted to be the one to cook the prime rib and turkey himself. He also brought some steaks for some of the guys who wanted barbecue. She didn't want to be under foot while he was in the middle of making his famous kitchen disaster zone, and he almost never offered to do the cleanup.

When the kitchen was tidy again, Sally asked her if she'd like a cup of tea, and Lydia agreed. They sat down at the dining table, reduced to half its normal size due to the traffic. Venom lay down at her feet.

"How's he doing with all this crowd?" Sally asked.

"He's a champ. He's got lots of distractions, though. But he's not seeming to mind at all. He loves the affection, he still gets to sleep with us at night, and we've gone through several nights now with no alerts and no barking. I think he's getting used to the routine and knows something is up, but he's not been signaling."

"You get to spend much time down in the garden?"

"I was going to today, but I just ran out of time. Thank you for your help. This is going to be great."

"No problem." Sally hesitated a couple of seconds while they both sipped their tea and watched the guys studying the wall of monitors, whispering amongst themselves. "You know, I was worried about you coming home."

"Why?"

"I really thought that maybe this would be something you and Harper couldn't maintain. He was such a mess after you left, and he's such a strong personality. I wasn't sure you would feel comfortable around him."

"I didn't at first, but we had a lot of time to talk back at D.C.. He really was very careful with me. He let me set the tone, and he didn't come over that often. No more than once a week. I finally got so that I was excited to see him. And, of course, from there it just sort of grew."

"Isn't that something? Here you fell in love with the

guy and don't even remember that person, that guy or the person you were when you fell in love with him. Now you're two new people together, and you fall in love all over again. I mean, it must be something more than personality. It has to be chemistry or something. Don't you think?"

"Definitely. I think it is. Like people say, it's written in the stars. Once I came here and I got to see where he lived—where I had lived and been so happy. I didn't remember it except flashes here and there, but I was at home. I was at peace."

"I'll tell you one thing, Lydia, he is so much in love with you. I don't think I've ever seen a man so smitten in my life. And he's not had an easy life. But he doesn't want to live if you're not in it. I thought we were going to lose him. I really did. Thank goodness he had Venom. Venom really looked after him. It was a special bond."

Lydia reached down and petted Venom's head, squeezing his ears and rubbing the bridge of his nose.

"Any luck on finding a dog?"

"Oh, yes, I didn't tell you. There's a rescue Dobie place down near San Francisco. And they called me and said they have a young female that is ready to be adopted. Apparently, she'd been not well taken care of, and she's been given a clear medical history. She's not damaged, but she was just neglected. She's a big dog, though. I think she'd get along great with Venom."

"I hope she's fixed."

"Oh God, yes, she is. I wouldn't want a girl dog in heat. Trust me on that."

"So when do you get her?"

"Three days, they said. They're going to bring her up to my vet here in Santa Rosa, the same one you guys go to. Dr. Gordon? And then he's going to give her a complete check-up, make sure everything looks good, and if everything does, then she's mine. I've got a nice bed for her. I've already bought her a bowl with pink flowers on it. It's really quite cute."

"You said big. How big is she?"

"Over a hundred pounds. She's four years old and very big for her age, but when they got her, she was pretty skinny. They've built all that up, and I think being in the country here, it will be really good for her muscle mass. I think she and Venom, if they get along, will be best friends and will have the whole run of your yard. Plus, on the occasion when you guys travel and you want to leave Venom with me, he will have a playmate. I think it's going to be great. I can't wait. A big change for me."

"I'm happy for you, Sally."

Lydia looked out the large windows into her gardens and sighed. "I feel like I can finally relax. You know, I was so tense about all of this, this whole operation.

"Still not over it, of course."

"No, I realize, but we have just this one more step to go through. After the interview with Lipori, I was feeling like there was no way we could control this. Now I have hope all will turn out. Am I being a Pollyanna?"

"Oh gee. Don't let me squash your hope. But maybe it's the calm before the storm. Don't let your guard down, kid. There's a lot ahead of you. These people are dangerous, but we have all the best guys around us. When it comes, it will be quick. It's the waiting that's the hard part for me."

THE DINNER WAS prepared and laid out on the dining table so that people could help themselves and sit out on the back patio or in chairs around the living room—wherever they could. Some monitored their consoles and ate prime rib, potato salad, and fresh green beans and other vegetables from the garden. Others sat and put their plates on their laps. A few sat at the dining room table.

Lydia hadn't met all the team, so one by one, they came over to her. Mallory Cruz was the first to join that group. She was an extremely attractive Latina lady, fit, who looked like she could take down anybody kickboxing or cage fighting, with jet black hair she wore in a braid down her back. She had large almond-shaped eyes and spoke with a slight accent.

"Nice to meet you. I've heard so many things about you, Mallory. Where are you from?"

"I'm from Puerto Rico."

"Harper tells me you got through BUD/S. That's a first, isn't it?"

"Yeah, I did. But I'm happier, I think, doing this, where I get to do what I do best. I would've liked to get picked for a SEAL Team, but they're not ready yet, and I have too much respect for them to push them. Someday, though. My second specialty would be wrestling. And I can also run, not quite breaking their records because I don't have the strength, but I was a track-and-field runner in high school and first two years of college."

"Are your parents here or in Puerto Rico?"

"They're in Puerto Rico. Very proud of me, though, and I've asked them to come visit, so if they do, you have to hang with me and my five sisters. They all want to come!"

"It's a deal. Can't wait. Where will you be stationed?"

"When you go outside and you turn around, look up the hill. You won't be able to see me, but I'll be up in that little gray and white water tower that you could just barely see at the top."

Lydia could barely make it out.

"From that place, I can see almost from Cloverdale nearly to Marin, maybe even as far as San Francisco if no fog. It's a huge panoramic view. And with my scopes, I can tell what you're eating on the back deck of your house. That's how good it is."

"Glad to have you."

Knute Thayer had been on one of Harper's teams earlier, and she had met him before but introduced himself to her anyway. Others step forward, including Paul Taylor.

Harper gathered them together all in one room and took the time to give a little speech.

"Well, ladies and gents, welcome to my house. Consider this a beach bonfire before a mission. You know what I mean."

The group laughed. Lydia knew the routine, the beach outings with the wives and kids before an important mission.

"I want you to know that both Lydia and I are incredibly grateful for you being an important part of our security, for coming together as this team. As you know, in two days' time or less, the authorities are going to come pick up Lipori, and we'll be given the location of the couple we're to intercept. Once we find out where they are, we will stage a pick up. Now we have to be conscious of the fact that they may be tipped off to what we're doing, and maybe they're gone already. We haven't heard from them in, what, five days now?"

He looked around the room, and several nodded their agreement.

"So from now on, I want you to keep your comms on day and night. I want you to sleep with them. I want you to make sure all your batteries are charged and your cell phones stay charged. I want you to make sure all your equipment is loaded and you have plenty of ammunition. If you need anything, if you all of a sudden run out of something, let me know, and we'll get it for you. You medics make sure you stay prepped in case we need you; you know the drill. We're going to try to keep everybody checked in for the handoff so you'll hear it as soon as we will, and that's going to start the clock ticking. Once he gives the address out, we've probably got no more than about five hours to get them. He has told us they are living nearby, but we are prepared for the fact that perhaps they're somewhere else. My intuition says they're close by."

The crowd agreed.

"I want you to keep Venom inside, so if he wanders out of a doorway, somebody grab him. He cannot go outside to the front, just a reminder, and in the backyard, I want him on a leash. I don't want to take any more chances. If he starts to alert, I want you guys to treat that as a warning sign and immediately fall into full action. He does not alert unless he has something to tell us. The other thing is, he is not to be fed off the table. We've trained him not to eat out of anything but his bowl. I had to train him so he doesn't pick up some kind of poison like he did the last time. Everybody clear on all that?"

"Are we allowed to use cell phones to call our families?" Sam Hobbs asked.

"Of course, Sam. You've got family down in Coronado, and some of you have family here. Make your calls tonight, just let them know you're not going to be available for a day or two, and give them the happy talk, okay?"

He paced the floor, adding one more point.

"If something should occur, we have all of your families numbers, and we will make sure they are informed right away if we have to leave the area. I'm thinking we're going to stay here. If we have to chase them, though, and apprehend them elsewhere, we will do that. This is a no-fail mission. We will find them. No excuses."

The pies were consumed, and Lydia along with Sally cleaned the kitchen and stacked meats on plates covered in foil so that guys could come in and help themselves to something or make themselves a sandwich during their shift. Sally had made five loaves of beautiful herb bread, and they left plenty of soft butter out in the kitchen.

It was late when Lydia decided to head to bed. Harper needed to coordinate a few things and call the admiral back east, so he promised he'd meet her later on upstairs.

Sally went home with the two guys who were living with her. She texted the all clear as did her two helpers, so the team didn't have to worry about her position being compromised. One by one, Lydia heard the check-in. The check-ins occurred once an hour. After the third one, she showered, slipped on a nightgown, and then removed her comm to prepare for bed. She set it on the night table.

Not much later, Harper came in, followed by Venom.

"You must be exhausted, Harper. It was a good meeting, but man can they pack it away."

He was focusing on undressing. "They're good guys, Lydia—the best I've ever worked with."

"You've thought of everything. All these monitors and recording devices. You have them patrolling as well?"

"Yes, ma'am. In addition to that, the guys that do patrol around the edges, they record as well. So we're like Fort Knox, Lydia."

He turned around on the bed and looked at her.

"And you're the prize. You're not bait, Sweetheart. You're the prize."

"I want to hear more."

"Let me take a shower, and then I'll tell you all my secrets."

"Oh, I can't wait."

CHAPTER 16

THE HANDOFF WAS performed just outside the prison gates in Murphy, Virginia. The guards, who were Patterson's Special Agents, confirmed it was indeed Lipori. The two Italian Federal Police officers were dressed in plain clothes, and after they presented credentials and took possession of Lipori, they had him handcuffed and secured to one of the agents. The guard reported the leg shackles were removed. That had not been in the agreement.

There was a black, unmarked car waiting to take them to the airport. Lydia knew he had a nonstop flight to Rome and then a puddle hopper to Florence. The two special guards informed the team the transfer was complete. As soon as he sat down in the car, the Italian policeman next to him in the backseat, he asked the guard to pull out a piece of paper in his shirt pocket. He had been dressed in street clothes, like the Federal Police, to keep the passengers on the flight calm, but the handcuffs would be obvious.

The guard opened it up and read into the comms the address in Kenwood of the couple. Everyone in their entire network heard it. Immediately, Lydia saw the monitors spring to life as keyboards researched the address, transmitting information about the surrounding area and owners and renters living nearby. This was done in a matter of seconds.

Harper hoisted up his duty bag over his shoulder, and he and five others left to go retrieve the couple. He gave her a quick kiss. "It all begins now."

"Break a leg."

"Ouch," he said as he exited their front door.

Everyone heard over the comms as Lipori told the guard, "Best of luck, Gents. I will see you the next time around. Ciao!"

Lydia noted the complete lack of panic in his voice, unlike before in the prison, and that alarmed her. She'd have to say he was even giddy.

The guard reported, "Okay, they're on their way to the airport, guys. They've got a tail. I also slipped a tracking device under Lipori's seat."

"We got it," said one of the techs in front of Lydia at the console.

It was confirmed to the guard. "You stay in touch with the tail. Let us know if anything happens," came the voice of Patterson.

As the car was driving away, everyone on the comms heard the guard say, "Asshole—not you, Admiral. Lipori. I hope I never see him again. If I do, it's because I went to hell."

A small cheer arose in the house at the prospect that Lipori was on his way back to Italy. Had they actually pulled this off? Somehow, it seemed all too simple.

Harper and the five in the Sprinter van verified their location and asked for a drone to be sent over the hill to Kenwood to help them out. One of Paul Taylor's NV drones was sent out, capable of traveling more than twenty miles per hour and able to record videos. It would be monitored by the house and arrive before the van did.

Others back at the house were using live map feeds, linked to county records so they had the location of the house, pictures of it and the neighborhood, and the names of all the neighbors nearby whether tenants or owners. They passed this down to Harper. There was a car in the driveway, a compact Ford. Also, a front porch light was on. It was a rural neighborhood without sidewalks. To Lydia, it all looked so normal—too normal.

Lydia listened as they chatted back and forth. The drone arrived before the team did. It did several sweeps up and down the street, showing little traffic at this time of night, but it registered all of the cars in the neighborhood including their license plates, which was downloaded to the team. The team was able to verify who was registered and who might be visitors. All the registrations were current and matched the vehicles. Nothing showed up as either a vehicle or home ownership in the couple's name. In fact, it showed an owner occupant living at that property, a Mrs. Barker. It did not appear to be a rental.

Harper received all this information and let them know he'd parked a block away. They spread out and surrounded the tiny house from all four sides. There wasn't time for a sniper, but Greg had brought his long gun anyway, just in case Harper needed him to get up on a garage or climb a tree. Before trying to enter, they needed to look inside. The go was given.

Harper carefully approached one of the windows on the east, since it appeared someone was in the living room watching TV.

"Poking my head in the dining window. I got one person in a lounge chair watching TV. Feet up. Looks like an elderly lady," said Harper. "Can't see her face."

"No one in rear bedroom," said another.

"Nothing in the kitchen. Can't see the bathroom."

"Looks like just her. Let's give her a wake-up."

The drone was allowed to hover lower, to get a good picture of the front door. Everyone in the house was seeing the whole act play out real-time on multiple monitors.

Careful to not make a sound on the porch, Harper knocked. And then he quickly backed away in case he was met with a volley bullets.

Nothing happened.

They pounded on the door the next time, using the owner's name. "Mrs. Barker? Are you there, Mrs. Barker?" Harper said outside the door. He put his ear to the window and didn't hear any movement.

He was given the all-clear to enter. He banged louder, asking for the owner again.

Next thing Lydia saw on the monitor was three of them breaching the front door and one coming through the back. They didn't use explosives since the front door wasn't even locked. Running into the living room with guns drawn, they found Mrs. Barker in the lounge chair. Everyone saw it as Harper described her.

"Gun shot wound to the head. Elderly white woman, about eighty. Appears to have been shot where she sat."

The body cam on Harpers bulletproof vest revealed a typed message on a piece of binder paper stuck to her chest.

"Goddamnit, we've been had," mumbled Harper.

Lydia heard the admiral ask him to read the note.

"'See you guys in hell. Don't wait up for me. I've

got things to do and places to go. Hope you have a nice day. My friends are much more valuable to me alive than dead. We're taking a little trip together, but see you soon! All my love.'"

The whole team burst into action. Lydia heard the admiral trying to get information from the guards who handed Lipori over.

The drone kept buzzing the whole area. Harper's team called the police, and as sirens began blaring, neighbors came out of their houses to look at the commotion. All five Silver Team members easily spoke to most of them, while keeping a lookout for any of their suspects who could still be lurking in the neighborhood.

"Give me some good news, Admiral," said Harper.

"Yes, the plane and the three men took off on time. They lost the tail, though, which concerns me. But I got verification he was checked in and on board. They would be landing in Rome in seven hours. The black car was abandoned at the drop-off. I'm checking with the terminal for a passenger manifest."

Several of the guys at the home called airport security to alert them and help with the manifest. Reports came back nothing unusual occurring, but Dulles was one of the busiest airports in the country.

Patterson got word to the airline company about the potential mishap. They reported no skirmishes or problems with the passengers. But they promised to alert the captain and stewardess so that, once they landed, they could land in a secure location and have the plane searched.

"What do you think, Admiral? Do you think he's really on that plane?"

"I'm more worried about the couple. I'd like to know where they are."

"To the home, be on your toes," said Harper. "Let's call the local Feds."

The admiral confirmed he was doing just that.

People continued to check the drones, looking for movement and vehicles driving through the neighborhood. Harper and the others were showing the couple's picture and asking people for sightings. Nothing came up. The whole neighborhood lit up when the coroner and the Kenwood Police arrived. Even more people came out into the street, clad in their pajamas and robes. The story given the Team was that Mrs. Barker was just a nice retired lady, well-liked, living by herself. She never had visitors, and she was just a regular. Just a no name face.

The perfect foil, thought Lydia. It was becoming all too perfect. The operation had thought of everything, and still these people had fallen through the cracks. But they weren't done yet.

Lydia was suddenly becoming more fearful each

minute that lapsed. It was turning out to be just as she had feared. She was beginning to doubt whether or not there was going to be anything they could do to confine him, to keep him from having his way however he wanted. He was two steps ahead of them in every sense. The coordination was masterful. She wished they had not boarded a plane that had to travel so far, because time was of the essence. The pilot wouldn't do an identity check with the plane mid-flight, especially flying internationally, so they would have to wait. She knew it was planned that way.

After the search in Kenwood and discussion with the police, Harper told the group they were coming back. The snipers checked in, Greg on top of the shed in the regional park said he saw some coyotes slide by, but no humans that he could tell.

One of the policeman called in, and it was patched into Harper's comm for all to hear, some information about an intruder that had been wandering the neighborhood that evening.

"So what was the report?" Harper asked.

"She just said that she saw some guy poking his head around the window. And when he saw her, he left. Later, she saw him lurking around Mrs. Barker's house."

"More than one or just one?" Harper asked.

"Just one. And he didn't have a car, either. He rode

a bicycle."

Someone announced, "That sounds like somebody living in the neighborhood. I'll bet they're still there."

"So we're going to change this, guys. We're gonna stay and continue looking," said Harper.

"Roger that," said one of the kids at the monitor in the living room.

While the house was buzzing with juice and tons of energy, Harper and the five guys cleared the roadway, examined several vacant homes, and even checked people's backyards when people were too afraid to go outside and check themselves. They looked at garages; they checked inside vacant cars, RVs, one boat, and a few campers. Most of the neighborhood dogs were barking their lungs out. The coroner left with Mrs. Barker's body, but the crime unit was working over the house carefully, collecting clues. Harper was obliged to turn over the note, but he took a picture of it first and was promised DNA evidence after they'd had it tested for prints.

Three hours went by, and with no specifics and no clues, it was becoming a dead end. They had questioned most of the neighbors with few exceptions. There was little else to do. So the team decided to come back to Bennett Valley.

Seconds later, Venom alerted. He started barking, dashing around in circles, wanting to go out the front door.

"Venom, he's coming back. Daddy's coming back. Is that what you're looking at?" asked Lydia.

One of the boys asked Harper how far away was. He was nearly twenty minutes away, not close enough for Venom to alert. The kid looked at Lydia. She could see the fear. Her whole world changed in that instant.

Lydia reached out to him. "Harper, Venom's alerting. Something's going on here. Get your butt back, but watch yourself, okay?"

"Will do. Have the guys ask the birds if they see anything."

She was confused but heard someone checking in.

Both Mallory and Greg confirmed. The report was negative.

"Anybody check on Sally?" Mallory asked.

"Brandon and Gordon, you guys up?"

The silence was stunning.

No one returned that call.

CHAPTER 17

L YDIA GRABBED HER cell and called Harper.

"Hey there."

"Remove your comms."

"What?"

"Remove your comms."

She heard the rustle movement on her earpiece. "Done. What's up?"

"They're at Sally's. That means they have comms. They are hearing everything we're saying. Get your guys silenced."

Rory, one of the young techs, whispered to her, his earpiece removed, "They should still chatter like normal. We don't want them to know."

"Did you hear that?"

"Yes. Done. Shit!"

Rory was passing information along the line with the men watching the monitors. Cell phones were out, and texting was fast and furious. He came back seconds later with a written note stating he'd gotten hold of Patterson. She nodded and let Harper know.

"Patterson says they should ditch the van. It's probably got listening devices planted, unless they checked before they took off."

Again, Lydia asked if he'd heard.

"Yes. Will do. Okay, gotta run. We're on our way."

They all heard Harper's foul-mouthed tirade on their comms. "Shit guys, we got a blowout. I'm going to be late. Everyone stay in touch, hear? We're on foot now, just outside of Kenwood."

Lydia knew it was the perfect ruse.

One of the techs gave his phone to Lydia. The admiral was on the line.

"I've issued orders to stay put for now. Let Harper and his five guys get to your location. But be ready to defend. I don't have the snipers. Can you make sure they're focusing on Sally's? If anyone attempts to leave, they need to be stopped from afar. Get my drift?"

"Yessir, I will."

"And, Lydia, good thinking."

She was amazed he was so calm under this kind of pressure. "I appreciate that, sir. Actually, it was Mallory who thought to check on Sally. But I'm glad I could help."

"Okay, we're gearing up for the landing in about an hour. Gotta go. You make sure to call this number if anything changes."

"Will do."

Her heartbeat slowed way down as her body cooled, preparing herself for a battle, perhaps. She and one of the techs double-checked the windows and doors. They asked for a report from the snipers, and it came back negative. They were tracking both houses now.

Venom had calmed down but was lying down in front of the entrance, waiting, listening. She knew better than to take him outside, but he'd need to go soon if she didn't.

She ignored the chattering until she heard a little scream and thought she detected Sally's voice. Everyone at the consoles began to chatter. They purposely gave messages to the two men with her, Brandon and Gordon, to throw the others off.

"Hey, Brandon. We know you're on the pot this morning. It doesn't take an hour to take a shit, man," Paul said, casually. "Please check-in."

"Goose, Sally fixing bacon for breakfast? I'm needing some right about now," he said to Gordon. He shrugged his shoulders and looked back at Lydia.

"Don't know if it will work, but gotta try."

She agreed.

Harper called her to let them know they found a farmer who lent them his ATV, and although it wasn't very quiet, they'd be over the hill in about ten minutes. Lydia told him nothing showed up yet, but she thought she heard a cry for help, perhaps from Sally. "Or she's been injured."

Just then, Mallory used the comms. "Hey, guys, we got lots of coyotes over here. You be careful out there. Those guys are so cunning. They're liable to hitch a ride on one of your drones, so don't send 'em out, okay?"

The veiled message was that they were on the move.

Greg answered. "Got it. Quit looking for coyotes and do your job, Mal."

"Asshole," came the voice over the comms. Then they all heard a shot ring out. Greg was staring at a screen showing Sally's garage as several people were herded into one group, attempting to get into Sally's car. The people weren't hurt, but Mallory had done a good number on the passenger side front tire. That vehicle would not be drivable.

Now alerted, the group quickly fell back to the house and disappeared.

She called Harper. "They've got them pinned down. We don't know who's there, but they can't get away in a disabled vehicle, thanks to Mallory."

"Awesome. We're almost there."

Venom squealed and ran to the back door. Two

fully armed men shut down the lights inside to keep the intruders from seeing inside. Nothing they could do about their double monitor wall, though, so a blue light still lit up the room.

They wore vests and helmets with NV goggles, slipping out the back door. Venom wanted to run with them, but Lydia held him back. He was anxious to get out there and go after the source of his concern.

They stopped the chatter. Greg came up to Lydia with a whisper. "They want to release the dog. You okay with that?"

She looked at Venom, who sat at her feet, totally focused on her eyes, begging for the chance to track. It would break her heart if anything happened to the dog. She had to rely on his training, on her faith that he'd be smart enough to get to someone before he got hurt. She didn't have time to call Harper and ask for a second opinion. She had to act and act now.

"Let's do it."

The door opened a few inches, and Venom made space through it and dashed off the deck, stealthy in his pursuit of something out there. Two shots rang out, but they heard Venom grab hold of something.

One of the Team fired. The dog was still making good work out of wrangling someone until one member arrived, and the noises ceased.

She didn't want to call out for him. She really didn't

want to, but she heard him barking and running up the trail as fast as he could, toward the back door of the house. He leapt into Lydia's arms. His teeth and mouth were covered in blood, but the dog was ecstatic. The whole team cautiously checked him over and gave him kudos he gladly accepted.

Greg was watching out for his teammates, and finally, they returned. They had the couple, both wearing military grade gear, including tactical vests. The man had taken a kill shot to the head, and the woman was screaming in pain, her left arm and neck mangled by the dog.

Lydia was on the phone to Harper.

"We're right outside Sally's house. That's great news." He hung up.

Harper left his comms on so the rest of the team could listen. He'd cornered Lipori in the garage. The terrorist threatened to shoot Sally, who was draped over him, apparently unconscious.

Lipori also wore an earpiece. Lydia thought this was all staged like some kind of passion play. But of course, Lipori, ever the overly confident evildoer, could never envision he could lose this little battle, not without taking a whole bunch of people with him.

She knew he would try to take Harper.

Except he had one flaw. He wanted to live, unlike some of the jerks he trained. He was no suicide terrorist. He enjoyed living too much. He would never get rid of the grip he had on the chance to make other's lives miserable, pawns in his own horror movie.

One of the five Team Guys confronted Lipori, giving him a moment's distraction as he turned without his coconspirators behind him, and Harper took the shot. In the millisecond before he pulled the trigger, there was silence. And then they all heard it.

"One giant kill for all mankind," he said.

CHAPTER 18

L YDIA DIDN'T GET to see Harper for almost a half an hour, as the Team gathered their things and made arrangements for transportation of the bodies and the patient. She would find out later that Sally had been knocked around a bit, the last blow so hard it left her unconscious. But she awakened later with a splitting headache, and they suspected a concussion. She had been bound and gagged and thrown in the same room as Gordon and Brandon, who had been chained and handcuffed. After being freed, Harper told her the worst injury was pulling the duct tape from their eyes and their mouths. Luckily, nobody was seriously hurt.

Lydia knew she was going to need to spend time with Sally. It had been such a harrowing experience, and Lydia knew how disoriented and how unstable her mental state was going to be.

When he walked through the door, Harper was sweaty and dirty from riding the ATV across the hill, over five miles. He was covered in grass stains, mud, and blood. He had cuts on his arms and fingers, having taken most of the brunt of it, being the driver. The rest of his guys were either on the miniscule flatbed in the way back or the second seat behind him.

She ran to him and swung her arms around him, sweat and all.

"I was so worried this time, but I knew you would be okay. I knew you were going to get there in time."

Exhausted, he'd leaned into her to accept the weight of her body and shook his head, dropping his bags and equipment. Someone quickly took his M3. Still clutching her with one arm, he attempted to unload his vest and then gave up. But he was still holding her tight against him.

Greg brought him a glass of ice water, which he downed in one long swig.

"It was close. That was really close."

The group reacted with a combination of hooyahs and favorite swear words.

"I'll never underestimate these guys again. What was I thinking?" he said this to the entire room, not just Lydia. His heart was beating fast, and she didn't want to cling too fiercely to him, so she let herself slip away to give him space to remove his vest.

The room suddenly became celebratory. They were gladhanding and shaking each other, slapping backs, and feeling good about the whole saga. Gordon and Brandon were welcomed as conquering heroes.

Paramedics arrived to take Sally to the hospital for a much-needed check up and asked if there was anyone else who also needed to go. Lydia asked Harper if she could accompany her. Of course, he gave his permission. She ran out to the rescue van and sat beside her neighbor.

Sally was also bloody, had a bruise above her left eye, and a cut on her forearm. She was wrapped in an orange blanket, holding a bottle of water.

"Hey there. Want some company?"

"Sure. Always room for more. You know, I thought I kind of liked doing all this. I think I'm second-guessing that now, Lydia. What do you think?"

"Let me put it this way, Sally. I don't think any of those deadbeat dads you see in court are going to stand a chance against you now. I mean, look what you've done!"

Sally leaned back with a cackle. It felt so good to hear her laugh.

"You know, that man of yours, he is one in a million, Lydia. If you ever dump him, I'm going to cross my own boundary and go after him my goddamn self. Don't you ever let that guy get out of your sight for a minute. He's worth all the heartache and pain, anything he could ever do to you in the future."

Lydia knew that was certainly true. She would forgive him for anything the rest of his life.

With one exception. She would never forgive him dying on the job.

THE HOSPITAL X-RAYED Sally, and luckily, she didn't have a skull fracture, nor did it appear she had a concussion. But she would be sore for several days. No stitches required, just some cleaning and butterfly strips. Her chest x-ray was clear as well. She'd been shoved around, but no ribs were broken. It did not appear she had any internal bleeding.

The doctor came over to Lydia and flashed his light in her eyes. She moved him aside with a frown.

"No, Doctor, I wasn't a hostage. I was just there. I was just part of the team back home, all safe and sound."

"Let me hear your heart," he insisted and placed the stethoscope against her chest and whistled. "Your heart's racing like a freight train. You sure you don't need to be checked out further? Chest x-ray?"

"No, I'm fine. Really."

"Humor me. I'm going to check to see what your iron counts are, because you look a little pale to me. You've been sick lately? Do you get anemic?"

She remembered the couple of instances of being sick to her stomach, but the last two days, she'd felt fine.

"I did have an episode, just about a week ago now, but since then, I've been pretty good."

"How's your eating and sleeping?"

Sally laughed at the same time. She was sitting on the other side of the table.

"What's so funny about eating and sleeping?" the doctor asked.

"Because we've not done much of either. I mean, we had a big beautiful dinner, and then ever since that, it's been biting nails and staying up all night catching catnaps whenever we could. It's been a pretty stressful time, right?" she asked Sally.

"Every minute of it. But we loved it. Lydia and I are on the team for good," Sally continued.

"Well, I'm just gonna take a blood test anyway. I would feel better, and I understand you think you're feeling fine, but I am hearing a rapid heartbeat, and I'm seeing the lack of color to your skin, even with all that you've been through recently. We'll get some blood, and then we'll go from there. That doesn't mean you can't go home, and I know you have some wonderful family to get back to, so I won't keep you long."

She didn't have time to object. The doctor left, and a lab technician took blood from both of them.

"I feel like we're a couple of old soldiers here in the medic tent, and they're writing up something for us, patching us up so we can run out to the battle again. I've never done anything like this before, Lydia. Do you suppose in a past life I was some kind of an Amazon warrior priestess or something?"

"I can see you being that, Sally. You don't back down. You're stubborn. That's a good thing, and a lot of people don't appreciate that."

"Well, when you're fighting for things you believe in, you get that way. Sometimes, you ruffle feathers you shouldn't, and then you know what they say."

In unison, both of them said, "Better to ask for forgiveness than permission."

They both laughed.

Sally began, "I can see what they like about the life. And I understand how coming home and gardening and tending the dog and fixing plumbing and roofing and working on the car and paving the driveway and all that stuff—I can understand how that wouldn't be as exciting as what they get to do every day."

"But, at the same time, when you get to be older—"

"Watch it there, girly. I am old enough to be your mother, you know. But I'm not done. Just like Harper. He's not done either."

"Oh, I know that, Sally. Trust me, I will never forget that."

THE NEXT FEW days morphed together as teams came

in and packed up and stored all the equipment, labeling them so they could use them on future ops. Patterson himself flew out and surveyed the house where all this activity took place. He met Sally, and Lydia watched how easily he could be a charmer. Even Sally was blushing.

Then he turned to Harper. "Next time, I'm going to veto your idea about setting up home base at your house. It just puts you and the whole family into much harder circumstance. I know you thought a lot about this, and this time it worked out. Next time, you'd probably need to relocate everybody. You want to do this away from Lydia and all the things that you hold there."

"Sir, I would love to, but I don't think she would've let me," he answered.

"You're darn right. I'm part of this now. Besides, I wouldn't trust anybody but him for my safety."

"I appreciate that, Lydia," said Patterson. "And you are an asset to this team. It's a matter of training, and we can't be putting civilians in harm's way. Now I don't want you to sign up for the military or sign up for Silver Team. If you can just keep this guy in line, keep his head straight, and keep him thinking, you're going to do more for this team than anything else you could do. And I mean that sincerely. The support staff of a warrior is almost as important as all his training and the guys he fights with. So don't think you're being demoted here. You're needed, it's just in a different capacity."

Lydia scowled, and Harper put his arm around her. He looked up at Patterson. "We'll talk about it. Trust me, we'll talk about it," he said with a wink.

"Did you find out what happened at the airport?"

"You mean, who landed in Lipori's place? Turns out the Italians were on Lipori's payroll. They stopped the car before it made it to the airport. The guards were tranquilized and left in a rental car, replaced with new guards with fake credentials, and the guy they escorted to Rome had thought he was just playing a part for a fiancé to propose to his lovely lady at the airport. He was part of the play. Surprised when he was taken into custody."

"That's a story he'll tell his grandchildren."

"Can you imagine how someone would agree to go on a free vacation in handcuffs?"

VENOM WAS EXCITED to be able to run through the garden by himself again. They did a careful sweep of all the access paths. The whole front yard near the gate was scraped and replanted with new soil just in case they'd missed some of the poison. The backyard had grown weeds, and there was vegetable bounty they hadn't picked for several days. After a back-breaking day pulling weeds, they took a time out and sat on the back porch watching Venom forage, looking for something to be interested in on his way to taking a pee.

"I never thought I'd share my bed with not only a beautiful woman but a hundred-pound dog who loves to cuddle. Can you believe that, Lydia?"

"I think it sounds perfectly normal. Why, what did you think you would be doing at this point in your life?"

He stared up at the sky, searching the clouds.

"I'll think on that one, Lydia. I'm going to keep my mouth shut so I don't get in trouble. There are some things between a man and his lady that just should not be said."

He smiled after the fact.

Later that afternoon, Lydia got a call from the hospital. She waited for the doctor to come on the line.

"I got your metabolic panel back, and I am happy to tell you that your protein, your iron, your overall blood results came out completely normal. Even your glucose level is normal, which is always something we start looking at after thirty. But there was one little thing I thought I'd like to mention to you, just in case you didn't know."

She held her breath. She hated how doctors had a real non-confrontational way of revealing bad news.

Was this going to be bad news?

"I'm ready. Hit me with it."

"Well, I'll just come out and say it. You're pregnant, Lydia."

Her stomach lurched again. Sunlight in the kitchen hurt her head, and she was light-headed immediately, just like that time at the prison. She was going to be sick again, and she felt herself fading away.

"Harper!" she yelled for him outside, holding on to the countertop to keep herself from falling.

He came running, holding her up and grabbing the phone.

"Hello? Who is this?"

"I'm Dr. Punjab. I saw your wife last night at the emergency room?"

"Yeah?"

"Is she okay?"

"What did you tell her?"

"I'm not sure I have permission to do so, but she has some news for you. I would ask her to give that to you right away. You can call me back if you like."

"Fuck this," Harper said with a sneer. He hung up the phone. "What the hell was that all about? Are you okay? Going to be sick again? Tell me what he told you."

He helped her sit down on a dining room chair and ran for a glass of water. She swallowed it all, took a deep breath, and looked up at him.

"Oh no, Lydia, is this serious?" he asked, emotion melting all over his words. He knelt in front of her and grabbed her hands, squeezing, nearly to the point of tears. "Tell me. What is it, sweetheart. I'm here, no matter what!"

"We're going to have a baby, Harper. Did you ever think that would happen?"

Now Harper's face was pale. His expression showed her he'd never expected to have this conversation, and he was clearly scared. "Oh, and how do you feel about that?"

She put her hands on either side of his face. "How do you think I feel, Harper? I'm delighted. Please, please tell me you are too."

His face lit up in a broad smile. He kissed her. Whispering to her lips, he said, "Absolutely. This is chapter two, sweetheart. I can't wait for the next adventure with you."

PLAY DATE

S ALLY WAS ABLE to pick up her female Dobie a few days after everyone went home. Her strength had fully returned, her head wasn't hurting any longer, and life appeared, except for upcoming interviews she'd have to submit to, back to normal.

Lydia and Harper were excited to have their first play date with Venom.

"Bring her by in the afternoon," said Lydia after Sally called her. "How is she?"

"She's a love. She follows me around everywhere. I'm almost tripping over her all the time. Loves the garden and likes to chase butterflies, like Venom."

"I've heard her bark, so I knew it was working out," said Lydia.

"Are they always this possessive? Literally, I can't do a thing without her right next to me, watching every little thing I do. I put away the dishes and she walks back and forth with me the couple of steps from the dishwasher to the cabinet, watches me take things out of the refrigerator to prepare, not just her meals but mine too. And the bathroom? Does—"

"Yes, he does. It's crowded when all three of us get in there."

"She's not yet socialized, so we'll have to watch their reactions, but she's completely well, had all her shots, and a course of precautionary treatments. Healthy as an ox, they say. Her coat has become so shiny since I last saw her. She's healing fast."

"And she's fixed, right?" Lydia had to ask just to be sure. Their Venom wasn't.

"Oh, yes. No worries there. We don't need to give Venom any consternation over that. I'm sure you guys are not in the mood for babies."

Lydia laughed to herself. She decided to wait to tell Sally the news.

It was a warm day, lots of sun and puffy clouds, so the heat level wasn't oppressive. Venom was standing by the front door when Sally drove up in her brand new SUV. He started to squeal when he saw a large Dobie sitting next to her in the passenger seat. She sat tall and straight, her eyes keenly focused on him as well.

Sally got out, came over to the passenger door, attached the leash, and took the dog out, walking her up to the front door.

Venom went berserk, howling, turning in circles, alerting to her presence, and checking Harper and Lydia's expressions. They stood back, Harper sipping on a whiskey, and watched the drama unfold.

"Should we put a leash on him?" Lydia asked.

"It's his house. He deserves to be free, as long as he doesn't abuse the honor. Let's see how he reacts first."

For a few seconds, both dogs stared at one another through the glass, neither moving a muscle, and then Lydia opened the door and let Sally and the dog enter.

Venom was squealing, sniffing her all over. Sally had a good grip on the leash, so the dog stood erect and accepted his investigation. Venum gruffed and showed a few of his top teeth by rolling back his upper lip, but the dog didn't flinch, just slowly turned her head to face him nose-to-nose.

She was nearly his size.

Then Venom did the typical behavior he always did when he wanted to run or play. He leaned over onto his front legs with his butt in the air, wagging his stub of a tail, and barked. She stepped back and then whined. On the leash, she did a complete dancing turn while Venom watched her. He leaned forward and barked softly, and she squealed. While Venom was sniffing her nose and face, he noted some scars over her eye and on her snout. He licked them gently.

It brought everyone to tears.

Sally kept the leash firm.

"What's her name?" Harper asked.

"Medusa," answered Sally. "Right, girl? You're Medusa."

The dog stoically peered up at her.

"But I'll call her Maddie. I just thought Medusa would be a good compliment to Venom. Snakes and all," giggled Sally.

Lydia hadn't seen her so happy.

"Well, let's see if they can be good neighbors. Does she know her name yet?" asked Harper.

"We're working on it."

"Hey, Maddie, want to go outside?" Harper said, kneeling down and extending the back of his hand.

Venom reacted immediately, barking, twirling, running over to the back door in anticipation of a run. Maddie licked Harper's hand and allowed him to pet the top of her head. "You're such a good girl. You have a wonderful mama."

Sally followed Harper over to the door, while he opened it and let Venom out. Venom didn't run down through the rows of plants and flowers but stayed back on the deck, still presenting his play stance for her, butt in the air again, and waited.

"You want to go play, Maddie?" Sally asked her.

She squealed and pulled against the leash. Sally made her sit first. She detached the leash and spoke softly, "Okay, girl. Go outside. Play with Venom."

That's all it took. Medusa shot out of the room and nearly hurdled the back deck in one lurch. Her strong legs took her down the garden pathway, right behind Venom. The two barked, barking at the plants and at each other, danced, and began to wrestle, stop, wrestle again, and then took turns chasing each other.

"I can't believe it," said Sally. "Like they were made for each other."

"I never had a doubt," said Harper. "He's been looking for a girl to share his life with for years, I think. And man, I know just how happy he feels."

LATER, THEY SHARED their news as all three of them sat out on the deck, Sally and Harper sipping whiskey while Lydia sipped her ice water.

"I'm not surprised," said Sally. "A father, Harper? I can see you doing that and doing it fantastically. Just like everything else in your life. Now this will keep you young. I've had friends who've had children late in life, and it does do that."

"I can honestly believe that, Sally."

She asked about the woman who had been captured and injured by Venom the night of the takedown.

"Maria is recovering in a prison hospital, awaiting a real extradition to Italy, although we're trying to get permission to try her here. With Lipori gone, I doubt she has the connections, so in Italy, she would certainly serve time, at least that's what Patterson says," said Harper.

"Has she given up any of their resources or revealed any names?" asked Sally.

"If I knew, I couldn't tell you. You understand."

"Of course. No problem."

"But my understanding is she's set on revealing nothing. She does already have an attorney, and they're pushing to get her out of the U.S., her team."

"She has a team? Wow. She's connected then," Lydia said with surprise.

"Could just be posturing with the Italians. No country wants to see its citizens being manhandled by another country's assets, but this is different than the extraction we did on Silver Team. This was done on American soil. For that, she'll most certainly have to stand trial. But we'll see. These things are complicated. We call them cleanups. We never liked to get involved with any of those on the Teams. No different now. Our job is done."

"Patterson did tell us they didn't think their team was very large, that they had just been getting started," said Lydia.

"So be vigilant, but not to worry then?"

"Nothing is a sure thing, but we think we got everybody. This time."

That was the elephant in the room. Lydia knew no one could really know when the next attack could occur. Harper had told her how groups changed, morphed into new groups, changed leaders and even countries where they operated. She was well aware it was a cancer that would attack wherever it could, wherever they were most vulnerable.

But they had other things to focus on these days. Harper would be doing ops during her pregnancy, and they'd created a protocol so that Lydia was never left alone again in that event. They'd done everything they could for Plan A and Plan B and Plan C.

After that, it was all strength, anticipation, thinking on their feet, and a lot of luck. But with the new family coming and the love they shared between them, she knew they'd make it.

No one was going to ruin her happily ever after.

They said goodbye to Sally and Maddie, Venom appearing to be sad his new friend was leaving. They calmed him down with pets as they watched Sally back up, turn around, and drive home.

Harper did not see the text message from Patterson:

"Maria has escaped. Facetime me as soon as you get this."

Did you enjoy Loving Harper, Book 2 of the SEAL Brotherhood: Silver Team series? If you haven't already, please pick up Book 1, Something About Silver, and read how this beautiful love story began for Harper and Lydia.

For some of the background on Sharon's best-selling SEAL series, the original SEAL Brotherhood is available in a bundle, The Ultimate SEAL Collection #1, followed by the next 5 books in the series, Ultimate SEAL Collection #2

Other SEAL Series:
SEAL Brotherhood: Legacy
Bone Frog Brotherhood Series
Bone Frog Bachelor Series
Sunset SEALs

And many more. You can find them on my website: authorsharonhamilton.com

Nearly all her books are available for your listening pleasure on Audible, here.
audible.com/author/Sharon-Hamilton/B004FQQMAC

ABOUT THE AUTHOR

NYT and USA/Today Bestselling Author Sharon Hamilton's SEAL Brotherhood series have earned her author rankings of #1 in Romantic Suspense, Military Romance and Contemporary Romance. Her other *Brotherhood* stand-alone series are: Bad Boys of SEAL Team 3, Band of Bachelors, True Blue SEALs, Nashville SEALs, Bone Frog Brotherhood, Sunset SEALs, Bone Frog Bachelor Series, SEAL Brotherhood Legacy Series and SEAL Brotherhood: Silver Team. She is a contributing author to the very popular Shadow SEALs multi-author series.

Her SEALs and former SEALs have invested in two wineries, a lavender farm and a brewery in Sonoma County, which have become part of the new stories. They also have expanded to include Veteran-benefit projects on the Florida Gulf Coast, as well as projects in Africa and the Maldives. One of the SEAL wives has even launched her own women's fiction series under the pen name of Annie Carr. But old characters, as well as children of these SEAL heroes keep returning to all the newer books.

Under the pen name S. Hamil, she has a new Dystopian/Sci-Fi/Fantasy Romance, Free to Love. Book 1 of this 5-book series has been released: Free As A Bird. The story arc is about a future alternative universe where Androids are feared because of their AI capabilities that outpace human intelligence, and yet the hero, an android, may become the savior of the world, both human and other.

Annie Carr, Sharon's Women's Fiction author pen name, has just released her first two books in 2023, I'll Always Love You, and Back to You, in Sunset Beach stories. She is planning this to become a multiple-book series.

A lifelong organic vegetable and flower gardener, Sharon and her husband lived for fifty years in the Wine Country of Northern California, where many of her stories take place. Recently, they have moved to the beautiful Gulf Coast of Florida, with stories of shipwrecks, the white sugar-sand beaches of Sunset, Treasure Island and Indian Rocks Beaches.

She loves hearing from fans through her website:

authorsharonhamilton.com

Find out more about Sharon, her upcoming releases, appearances and news when you sign up for Sharon's newsletter.

Facebook:
facebook.com/SharonHamiltonAuthor

Twitter:
twitter.com/sharonlhamilton

Pinterest:

pinterest.com/AuthorSharonH

Amazon:

amazon.com/Sharon-Hamilton/e/B004FQQMAC

BookBub:

bookbub.com/authors/sharon-hamilton

Youtube:

youtube.com/channel/UCDInkxXFpXp_4Vnq08ZxM
BQ

Soundcloud:

soundcloud.com/sharon-hamilton-1

Sharon Hamilton's Rockin' Romance Readers:
facebook.com/groups/sealteamromance

Sharon Hamilton's Goodreads Group:
goodreads.com/group/show/199125-sharon-hamilton-
readers-group

Visit Sharon's Online Store:
sharon-hamilton-author.myshopify.com

Life is one fool thing after another.
Love is two fool things after each other.

REVIEWS

"Fans of Navy SEAL romance, I found a new author to feed your addiction. Finely written and loaded delicious with moments, Sharon Hamilton's storytelling satisfies like a thick bar of chocolate." —Marliss Melton, bestselling author of the *Team Twelve* Navy SEALs series

"Sharon Hamilton does an EXCELLENT job of fitting all the characters into a brotherhood of SEALS that may not be real but sure makes you feel that you have entered the circle and security of their world. The stories intertwine with each book before...and each book after and THAT is what makes Sharon Hamilton's SEAL Brotherhood Series so very interesting. You won't want to put down ANY of her books and they will keep you reading into the night when you should be sleeping. Start with this book...and you will not want to stop until you've read the whole series and then...you will be waiting for Sharon to write the next one." (5 Star Review)

"Kyle and Christy explode all over the pages in this first book, [*Accidental SEAL*], in a whole new series of SEALs. If the twist and turns don't get your heart jumping, then maybe the suspense will. This is a must read for those that are looking for love and adventure with a little sloppy love thrown in for good measure." (5 Star Review)

PRAISE FOR THE
BAD BOYS OF SEAL TEAM 3 SERIES

"I love reading this series! Once you start these books, you can hardly put them down. The mix of romance and suspense keeps you turning the pages one right after another! Can't wait until the next book!" (5 Star Review)

"I love all of Sharon's Seal books, but [SEAL's Code] may just be her best to date. Danny and Luci's journey is filled with a wonderful insight into the Native American life. It is a love story that will fill you with warmth and contentment. You will enjoy Danny's journey to become a SEAL and his reasons for it. Good job Sharon!" (5 Star Review)

PRAISE FOR THE
BAND OF BACHELORS SERIES

"[Lucas] was the first book in the Band of Bachelors series and it was a phenomenal start. I loved how we got to see the other SEALs we all love and we got a look at Lucas and Marcy. They had an instant attraction, and their love was very intense. This book had it all, suspense, steamy romance, humor, everything you want in a riveting, outstanding read. I can't wait to read the next book in this series." (5 Star Review)

PRAISE FOR THE
TRUE BLUE SEALS SERIES

"Keep the tissues box nearby as you read *True Blue SEALs: Zak* by Sharon Hamilton. I imagine more than I wish to that the circumstances surrounding Zak and Amy are all too real for returning military personnel and their families. Ms. Hamilton has put us right in the middle of struggles and successes that these two high school sweethearts endure. I have read several of Sharon Hamilton's military romances but will say this is the most emotionally intense of the ones that I have read. This is a well-written, realistic story with authentic characters that will have you rooting for them and proud of those who serve to keep us safe. This is an author who writes amazing stories that you love and cry with the characters. Fans of Jessica Scott and Marliss Melton will want to add Sharon Hamilton to their list of realistic military romance writers." (5 Star Review)

PRAISE FOR THE
GOLDEN VAMPIRES OF TUSCANY SERIES

"Well to say the least I was thoroughly surprised. I have read many Vampire books, from Ann Rice to Kym Grosso and a few other Authors, so yes I do like Vampires, not the super scary ones from the old days, but the new ones are far more interesting, far more human than one can remember. I found Honeymoon Bite a totally engrossing book, I was not able to put it down, page after page I found delight, love, understanding, well that is until the bad bad Vamp started being really bad. But seeing someone love another person so much that they would do anything to protect them, well that had me going, then well there was more and for a while I thought it was the end of a beautiful love story that spanned not only time but, spanned Italy and California. Won't divulge how it ended, but I did shed a few tears after screaming but Sharon Hamilton did not let me down, she took me on amazing trip that I loved, look forward to reading another Vampire book of hers."

"An excellent paranormal romance that was exciting, romantic, entertaining and very satisfying to read. It had me anticipating what would happen next many times over, so much so I could not put it down and even finished it up in a day. The vampires in this book were different from your average vampire, but I enjoy different variations and changes to the same old stuff. It made for a more unpredictable read and more adventurous to explore! Vampire lovers, any paranormal readers and even those who love the romance genre will enjoy Honeymoon Bite."

"This is the first non-Seal book of this author's I have read and I loved it. There is a cast-like hierarchy in this vampire community with humans at the very bottom and Golden vampires at the top. Lionel is a dark vampire who are servants of the Goldens. Phoebe is a Golden who has not decided if she will remain human or accept the turning to become a vampire. Either way she and Lionel can never be together since it is forbidden.

I enjoyed this story and I am looking forward to the next installment."

"A hauntingly romantic read. Old love lost and new love found. Family, heart, intrigue and vampires. Grabbed my attention and couldn't put down. Would definitely recommend."

"Dear FATHER IN HEAVEN,

If I may respectfully say so sometimes you are a strange God. Though you love all mankind,

It seems you have special predilections too.

You seem to love those men who can stand up alone who face impossible odds, who challenge every bully and every tyrant ~

Those men who know the heat and loneliness of Calvary. Possibly you cherish men of this stamp because you recognize the mark of your only son in them.

Since this unique group of men known as the SEALs know Calvary and suffering, teach them now the mystery of the resurrection ~ that they are inde-structible, that they will live forever because of their deep faith in you.

And when they do come to heaven, may I respect-fully warn you, Dear Father, they also know how to celebrate. So please be ready for them when they insert under your pearly gates.

Bless them, their devoted Families and their Coun-try on this glorious occasion.

We ask this through the merits of your Son, Christ Jesus the Lord, Amen."

By Reverend E.J. McMalhon S.J. LCDR, CHC, USN
Awards Ceremony SEAL Team One
1975 At NAB, Coronado